I0620745

The Christmas Memory

BARBARA WINKES

Copyright © by Barbara Winkes 2023 (Ebook), 2024 (Paperback)

All rights reserved.

This book is a work of fiction. Any resemblance to actual persons, living or dead, events or locales are purely coincidental. This book or any portion thereof may not be reproduced or used in any manner whatsoever without the express written permission of the author except for the use of brief quotations in a book review.

ISBN: 978-1-0690835-2-4

Created with Atticus

For D.

Chapter One

CLARE

"This is my stop, Mom. I have to go. Love you. Bye!" Clare slipped her cell phone into the pocket of her coat and got up from her seat. She had not lied—her stop was coming up next. She might have had a few more seconds, but they wouldn't have added anything new to the conversation. An important meeting with her bosses was first on the agenda, and she needed her head in the game, not feel worried or guilty about her choices.

The subway came to a halt, and she stepped onto the platform and hurried toward the stairs together with dozens of other commuters. Once she had escaped the busy hub, Clare could breathe a little easier. As usual, she and her team were well prepared for the meeting. When she had more time, she would make another attempt at explaining to her mother and the rest of the family.

Clare had made sure she left on time. Slowing her step, she smiled at the store windows and houses already decorated for

Christmas. Clare had fallen in love with the city when she first visited. Living and working here, especially around the holidays, was a dream and a blessing. She wouldn't change a thing—except maybe her family's persistent efforts to make her come home to Havenwood.

She had yet to figure out how to tell them that the city was now her home, without disappointing them. After a little over a year, she couldn't be happier.

Okay. Perhaps she could...but that was another story, highly unlikely to come true.

Together with a man in a suit and a couple of women looking eager to start their sightseeing trip, she crossed the street at a light and toward the entrance of Jay & Parker. Lost in thought, Clare didn't notice the small patch of ice until she stepped on it and lost her balance for a few, terrifying seconds. One of the women who had been waiting at the light reached out to steady her. Clare turned around to give the concerned stranger a smile.

"Thank you. That could have been much worse."

"Are you all right?"

"Yes. Perfect. Thanks."

A little more rattled than she'd like to admit, Clare went up the stairs and opened the door to the lobby, heading straight to the right where the coffee shop *The Ground Floor* was located. She hadn't been nervous until now, but thanks to her meticulous planning, she had time for breakfast and a sweet concoction to calm her nerves.

A familiar calm settled over her when she saw Avery, her favorite barista, behind the counter. Together with the scents of coffee, vanilla and cinnamon, the sight went a long way to distract her from the almost catastrophe.

"Good morning. The usual, or can I tempt you into trying something new?"

Clare didn't know if Avery talked to other customers the same way, or if it got them flustered the same way, and she didn't care. The time between arriving at the building and settling behind her desk with the day's tasks was special and precious to her, and had been since before last Christmas.

"Those cinnamon buns look amazing," she said. "I'll have one...and I should have a black coffee with that."

"But...?" Avery prompted, a hint of mischief in her smile. She always presented a bright moment in Clare's day, at times, the brightest. Her parents had instilled the idea that a good breakfast was essential to starting the day right. They should be proud of her.

She realized Avery was still waiting for an answer.

"I'll go with a toffee nut latte today."

"Important meeting, right?" Avery asked as she got to work, which made Clare ridiculously happy. She had told her the other day. Avery had an excellent memory for these little things.

"Yeah. I should be okay, but...You never know."

"I'm sure you'll be amazing."

"That may sound conceited, but I have to be. At least somewhere in the area of amazing."

"No, I get you." Avery didn't miss a beat creating Clare's order. Clare knew that she did get her. Avery was a photographer who took on freelance jobs on a regular basis. One of them had been with Jay & Parker. Some of her work was exposed at *The Ground Floor*, but she had yet to get her big break.

Unlike Clare, Avery didn't obsess much about anything. It was refreshing.

"It might help convince your folks."

"I hope so," Clare returned. She had shared a lot over the past year, and she didn't even mind. They had gravitated towards each other from day one. "I'll need a convincing argument.

3

They are this close to inviting a new-in-town, single teacher to Christmas dinner."

"Good luck on both fronts." Avery gave her a quick, sympathetic glance.

"Thank you."

"Hey, maybe we should pretend to be girlfriends. Both our parents might stop asking us to come back?"

"Maybe." It was too early in the morning for the joke. Knowing Avery meant it as such was almost cruel. Not intentionally, of course. Avery would never do that.

"In the meantime...Here you go, and Happy Anniversary!"

Startled and intrigued by the small candle on the cinnamon bun, Clare didn't answer right away.

Avery's face fell, and she apologized hastily.

"Oh no, that was a bit too much. I'm sorry. I didn't mean to overstep. It's just that today is..."

"Of course. Thank you so much! I almost forgot about this. It's my lucky day. You're the best."

Who was overstepping now? Clare cleared her throat. It might be the light, or did she make Avery blush?

"Your first day on the job," Avery clarified. "One year ago. And thank you. I like to remember these things."

She was adorable when rambling. Clare blew out the candle, realizing with regret that she would have to cut the conversation short, and not just because of the customers that had come in.

"Look who's amazing. I'm afraid I have to get going but thank you for everything."

"You're welcome! Let me know how it went."

"I will," Clare promised, picked up her bun and coffee and left. She might have a few more minutes to stay at the coffee shop, but she needed to get ready, not be distracted.

When she was in the elevator, Sara, one of the copyeditors, stepped inside at the last moment.

"Oh, is it your birthday?" she asked.

"No. Just someone being kind."

"Well, it's the season," Sara reasoned. "Let's hope Jay & Parker will be as kind with the campaign."

Clare had nothing to add to that, and they rode to their floor in silence. For some time now she wished it could be more than kindness, that Avery, too, imagined they could be more than friends. Who was she kidding? She was falling for the person as sweet as the indulgences she served Clare most mornings. Usually, Clare wasn't shy about making the first move, but she had reason to hesitate. Too much time had passed, and they had established a comfortable pattern. She wouldn't want to lose a friend over a foolish idea. It wasn't worth it.

Simply unrealistic. She might as well be wishing on the perfect star Avery had decorated her latte with.

Chapter Two

AVERY

Given that *The Ground Floor* was located in a tower downtown, it was always busy, more so during the holidays when residents and tourists alike needed their share of caffeine and breakfasts, lunches and sweet treats.

Avery loved interacting with all of them, the energy they brought, their stories. She had spent a little more time and attention on Clare, the copywriter for Jay & Parker who had moved to the city last year.

She didn't have much time to think about her during the day, but she had been on Avery's mind more than most regulars, enough that Max, one of her colleagues and roommates, had noticed.

"The candle was a cute touch," he remarked as he folded his apron. "But I think you'll have to be a little more obvious than that."

"I don't know what you're talking about," Avery said, feeling like she'd gotten caught with her hand in the proverbial cookie jar. Funny since they were surrounded by actual baked goods.

"Oh, I think you do, my friend. You have to make a move sometime, or let it go. Everything else would be..."

"Pathetic?" For a split-second, she had forgotten that she had no intention of confiding in him.

"I wasn't going to say that. But you should do something."

"True. I should finish up here and go home. Don't worry. I got it."

"Are you sure? I could help..."

"No, you go. I'm almost done. See you later."

"Chantal and Ryan wanted to go out for drinks later. Are you coming with us?"

Avery loved all her roommates, the way she loved everything about the city, but she spent a lot of time with them already. She didn't say it out loud, but a quiet evening at home, especially after talking to customers all days, sounded nice. Wondering what Clare was doing tonight, she suppressed a sigh.

Probably celebrating the big project she had been working on for weeks, drinks, with colleagues, perhaps someone special...Max did have a point. She couldn't go on like this forever—or could she? If Clare wasn't interested, things could become incredibly awkward. And why would she be when *she* hadn't made a move either? Some dreams had better stay just that, a dream. It wasn't like she was unhappy.

Avery cast a glance at the photographs on the wall. Thanks to her boss, she had been able to showcase them here, and even sold a respectable number of them.

The thought brought back the joy and excitement that had been waning. Clare had been one of the first customers to ask about her work, and to buy a couple of black-and-white impressions of the city.

Avery had nothing to complain about. Her favorite holiday was coming up and she had nothing but gratitude in her heart.

That was, until she locked *The Ground Floor* and headed to the front doors of the building. How ironic was it that she recognized the back of Clare's dark blue coat on the steps, a few paces ahead of her? She seemed in a hurry, probably hoping to catch the next subway, or eager to meet up with friends...a friend...

A few snowflakes were drifting in the air, not enough to stick. The temperature had dropped to a harsh point though. Avery buttoned up her coat all the way and arranged her scarf. Gratitude for everything she had quickly turned to shock when she saw Clare slip and fall only a few feet away from the last step. Without thinking, Avery ran to her side, barely avoiding the same fate. When she dropped to her knees next to her, a group of bystanders was already forming.

"Clare! Are you okay?" Cell phone in hand, she called 911, frantically scanning her friend for injuries. Her eyelids were fluttering. She would probably have a raging headache. Avery prayed that it wouldn't be worse. "Please, stay with me. I got you." She took off her scarf and carefully slipped it under Clare's head.

"Yes. I have an emergency. My friend slipped on the sidewalk and hit her head. Please send an ambulance."

When she had given all the necessary information and was assured that help was on the way, Avery brushed her hand over Clare's forehead, relieved when she saw her blink.

"Oh, this can't be good..." With a frown, Clare struggled to sit up.

"No, please, don't move. The ambulance will be here soon."

"Ambulance?" Clare repeated, sounding confused. "Where are we?"

"You fell, but don't worry. We'll get you to the hospital in no time."

This elicited a faint smile from Clare.

"Can't you just take me home? I think I'm fine. Let's make it a relaxed quiet evening?" she asked, sounding hopeful.

Avery had no time to deal with her own confusion, as the paramedics arrived and took over.

"Ma'am, please step aside."

She hurried to oblige, nearly bumping into one of the bystanders.

"Avery…"

"Yes, I'm here."

Avery's jaw dropped when Clare, now on a gurney, reached out to take her hand, her grip surprisingly tight.

"Can she come with me?"

"I'm afraid there's no room. We have to go. You can follow us to the hospital."

"Is there really no room, or do you treat straight injured people differently?" Clare closed her eyes, her features tensing with pain. "Okay. I'll see you in a bit."

"Yes. I'll be there as soon as I can."

After making sure she knew where the paramedics were taking Clare, Avery headed to the next subway stop, her mind still reeling with what she had witnessed.

To her relief, Clare seemed mostly okay, but Avery still couldn't make sense of her statement. Straight people?

It didn't mean anything. The incident had to be scary for her too, and in that moment, Avery was the closest thing she had to a friend. A friend who would be there for her.

She arrived at the hospital twenty minutes later, and, with renewed determination, went to find Clare. Waiting anxiously until the nurse at the front desk gave her the information, Avery reasoned that Clare had been thinking ahead. They wouldn't give access to a total stranger?

She didn't have to make anything up though, and a few minutes later, she snuck behind the curtain where Clare was sitting on the bed, looking lost. Avery's heart went out to her.

"I'm so sorry it took so long," she blurted out.

Clare's demeanor changed drastically when she saw her. She all but beamed.

"It's fine. You're here now. Wow, I'm sorry about that. This is not how I planned for the evening to go. Come here."

Reluctantly, Avery stepped closer, perplexed when Clare folded her in a firm hug. Too many sensations and emotions came at her all at once, even more so when Clare pulled back and kissed her lips softly.

Was she the one who had hit her head? This couldn't be real.

Behind them, someone cleared their throat.

"I'm Dr. Mason," the woman in the lab coat said. "You must be Avery."

"I...um...yes. That's me. Nice to meet you." Avery cringed, but no one seemed to notice.

"Your girlfriend was very lucky," Dr. Mason announced.

The relief nearly made her knees buckle.

Wait...what?

"I'm glad to hear that, but—"

"I told you she'd be so worried," Clare chimed in. "Can I go now?"

"Remember you have a mild concussion. Watch out for the symptoms..."

"Yes, I know. I won't be alone, and I promise, we'll be right back here if anything happens. I'd really love to go home." Clare cast a hopeful gaze at Avery, who nodded.

"I'll call us a cab," she confirmed. "Dr. Mason, could I talk to you for a second?"

"Of course."

If her lips were still tingling from that kiss, that meant she didn't imagine it, or did it? Outside the curtain, the doctor spoke first.

"I know this probably looked scary, but I can assure you, Ms. Hartley will make a complete recovery. Some small memory gaps are normal under the circumstances."

Small? Avery was starting to think that Clare wasn't just holding on to the story for the hospital staff. No one had tried to stop Avery from seeing her, so...How? *Why?*

"That's good to hear. I was wondering, should I tell her? I mean...If she gets things wrong?"

"I would advise you to be patient. Like I said, she'll be fine, but even a small disruption of recollection can be upsetting. Give her some time. From what she told me, you'll do just fine."

The heat rushed to Avery's face as she wondered what exactly Clare had told the doctor. It didn't matter. She could be patient all right. Clare might be confused, but she needed someone to be with her right now, and Avery would be that person.

They could sort out everything else later.

"Thank you. She went back to the room where Clare was waiting for her.

"Let's get you home," she said, hoping to sound like eternally optimistic Avery that Clare had come to know. The last thing she wanted was to upset her.

It was lucky that sometime in the past year, Clare had given her a business card, so she could give the cab driver the right address.

Chapter Three

CLARE

She had so many questions, most of which aggravated the headache that had already been abating. Clare was willing to go with the doctor's orders to have some peace. No double vision. No nausea.

Lucky. Having Avery watch over her, arriving at the right moment, made her the luckiest person of all.

She needed something good, because from one moment to the next, her world had become unexpectedly distressing, the hospital visit and fading headache the least of it. The circumstances of her fall were vague and grey. She remembered being on her way to work, talking to her mother, and then...nothing. Thank God Avery had been nearby.

She suppressed a smile, aware that Avery was watching her every step as they got out of the cab and walked to her front door.

"I'm so glad I remember home," she said, surprised by the flash of panic on Avery's pretty face. Even stressed like she appeared now, she was adorable.

"That's a good thing," Avery eventually agreed.

"Yes. That means I have an address to give to the delivery guy. I feel like I'm starving! Would it be terrible if we had pizza...and waffles?" She almost regretted her words when she saw the renewed panic on Avery's face and frowned. "It's not the first time I have strange food cravings, right?"

She was rewarded with a soft smile.

"No, it's not, but that's fine. We'll get you everything. I'd be more worried if you were feeling nauseated."

"Just the opposite."

They went up in the elevator. Even if her mind still felt a bit clouded, Clare remembered without hesitation which floor to take, and which apartment her key would unlock. That was a relief.

She hadn't forgotten about the project either. A wave of dread came over her, and she halted in mid-motion before turning the key.

"I did go to the meeting, didn't I?"

"As far as I know, yes. I saw you go up, and the next time was when you...fell. Sorry."

"That's okay. We're okay. Deep breath."

Clare unlocked the door and let Avery in first. Despite the reassurances she had received from the doctor and from Avery, she was more shaken than she wanted to admit. At least they were home, in blessedly familiar surroundings. She looked down at herself, realizing the smear of dirt on the sleeve of her coat.

A case for the dry cleaners. Tomorrow. Dr. Mason had advised her to take a couple of days off which was tricky, given the new project. How difficult could it be? She wasn't operating heavy machinery. She could sneak in breaks...maybe. And there was always a coffee, a sweet treat and a smile waiting for her downstairs.

She stepped forward and enveloped Avery in a tight hug. Perhaps a little too tight judging from her resulting gasp. Clare couldn't help it. She'd never been so grateful for her—and she would never take her presence for granted again, not for a minute.

"Okay, how about I take a quick shower and then we can order something to eat? I'd really like to get into PJs first. What about you?"

"Me...? Oh, I'm good, thanks."

It occurred to Clare that Avery must be just as shaken to have witnessed her fall. Her next question confirmed Clare's assumptions.

"Are you sure you'll be okay in the shower? You don't feel dizzy?"

"Just tired. I swear. You could order dinner in the meantime?"

"I can do that."

Clare reached out to brush her fingers over Avery's cheek, amused to find her blush. She couldn't remember a time when she wasn't head over heels in love with her. How had she been so lucky to find someone this sweet?

"You still want pizza and waffles?" Avery asked, breaking the spell.

"Actually, whatever you like. Surprise me. It's all in your hands. Wow." Clare straightened. "I'm sorry for giving both of us quite the scare, but worst-case scenario, I lost a few hours of my day. It could have been so much worse. Let's not dwell. The most wonderful time of the year is almost here." She laughed. "Listen to me rhyme. I should really take that shower now."

"Okay. I'll come up with something."

"Thank you."

Clare was halfway to the bathroom, starting to unbutton her blouse when she heard Avery say,

"Clare. Please wait."

She turned around, struck by Avery's serious expression.

"What's wrong?"

"Nothing. I swear. Just holler if you need anything, okay?" Her smile looked a little forced. "I won't be far."

"I know. That's what you get for wanting to live in the city."

Clare left for the bathroom where she dropped the rest of her clothes and stepped into the shower, mindful not to let the water get too hot.

Something was still nagging at the back of her mind, but she did her best to ignore it. Food and sleep would do wonders, no doubt about it.

Chapter Four

AVERY

Was she doing the right thing? The doctor had said not to push Clare. Her memory could come back within hours, days, or not at all. Sure, a few hours in the day wouldn't make too much of a difference in the long run.

Something else would. Big difference. Was she a terrible person because part of her still wished it could be real?

Avery could be practical in the face of crisis, but she had no idea how to handle Clare's misconception. And her displays of affection. How was that even possible? What little Avery knew about amnesia was that it usually had to do with suppressing trauma. One challenging workday, a mild concussion, that couldn't be enough of an explanation, could it?

Clare wasn't pretending, which meant, at least in the present moment, she had actual feelings for Avery? Or she felt them because she thought she should, because she mistakenly believed they were together?

If those feelings were real, how would she react if she found out the truth? It was all too confusing. Whenever Avery reminded herself to rewind a few hours, she came to the same conclusion: Clare would have said something before. Anything.

What would happen if she told her the truth?

There was one thing that she *could* do for her. Avery looked up the site of one of her favorite restaurants in town and ordered the pizza special for two.

She stepped closer to the bathroom door, assured that the water was still running, and went into the kitchen.

Avery found everything she needed, and by the time Clare returned from the bathroom wearing a fluffy robe, she had her batter ready.

"Food is on the way," she said. "Waffles can be dessert or breakfast, depending on how hungry you are."

There were subjects she didn't dare to address yet. At least she could take care of the necessities. It was a lot easier than she'd feared. Clare was organized, and to Avery's pleasant surprise, she did own a waffle maker.

"Avery."

The unmistakable emotion on Clare's voice made her heart sink. She remembered. That was the only explanation.

"I'd understand if you wanted me to leave, but I'm not going to, at least not now. I promised the doctor I'd look after you."

Clare sat in a kitchen chair.

"It's not that. I realized...All of your things are gone. What else did I miss? Did we have a huge fight? Did we break up?"

Each of her questions felt like a gut punch. For some inexplicable reason, Avery couldn't stop stirring. For all of this, Clare deserved the most perfect waffles in history. She deserved the most perfect holidays.

"No," she said, feeling worse at Clare's instant, visible relief.

"Oh good. I'm so glad I'm sitting. I'm not sure what I was thinking."

"You've had a rough day. But, we don't live together." That was the truth, and somehow it fit into a lie. Confusion didn't even begin to cover it. Avery tried to rein in her runaway emotions. She didn't want to upset Clare who had been tearing up at the idea of their imaginary break-up. She didn't want to waste time wondering how it could be possible. "Not yet," she added.

"Okay." Clare wiped a hand over her face. "I'm warning you, I might be acting a little strange for the next few days. But I know this. I'm hopelessly in love with you, I'm good at my job, and Christmas is my favorite holiday."

"I can see that," Avery acknowledged, grateful for the lighter tone. Clare's apartment was tastefully decorated, ready for the season. She wanted to say it back, because it was the truth, but she'd only get herself into more trouble down the line. "It's beautiful. And you're very loveable yourself." She hoped that was the right way to go.

"Thanks."

She didn't know how to interpret Clare's pensive gaze, so she went back to her preparation.

"Let me put this in the fridge, and I'll make them later?"

"Sounds good. About those decorations..."

The sound of the doorbell interrupted her.

"I got it," Avery declared and hurried to the door. She paid the delivery guy whose eyes widened at the tip she gave him.

"Happy holidays," she said and took the box and a couple of bags from him before she carried everything over to the dining area.

Clare had been setting the table. Now she stood behind Avery, arms crossed over her chest. She looked like she was trying not to laugh. That was better than tears, Avery reflected, though she had to admit she might have gone overboard.

"You didn't invite a couple of friends over while I was in the shower?"

"No. I just wasn't sure what exactly…you were in the mood for, so I went with the combo. A few slices of different pizzas, fries, and salad." *What exactly you liked*, Avery had almost said, but that would be strange if they had been together for a while.

"This is great. Thank you. I can't wait."

"Well, you don't have to. Let's eat."

·♥·♥·♥·♥·♥·

Clare's appetite was surprisingly unaffected by her experience.

"This was great," she said. "You could have had some wine though."

"That's okay." It would have felt strange to Avery even if they had been together. But they weren't, and a nice dinner with wine…It was all too dangerous, too deep into the delusion. Listen to yourself. Here she was, at nine-thirty on a work night, making waffles for the woman she had been crushing on for months.

Coffee was brewing, and from the kitchen, she could see that the snow had intensified in the past few hours. Getting to work tomorrow would be a challenge. Could she?

She should have tried to reach Max, ask him if he could cover her shift. If Clare stayed home for a couple of days, Avery should stay with her, no matter how complicated things were.

Clare had switched on the Christmas lights sprinkled all over the living room and lit a candle. When Avery returned with a tray holding coffee and a stack of waffles, she froze for a heart-beat. She stood for several seconds, blinking back tears of her own.

The beautiful romantic atmosphere only intensified the pain, knowing it was all an illusion caused by...what? Wishing on a star? A concussion?

"There's no way I should still be hungry, but I am. And those look so good. Thanks for taking care of me." Clare's tone was so warm and affectionate—appropriate when directed at your loved one—it made her want to cry even more.

"Of course," she managed.

"Come on. Sit. We can relax a bit. Make it an early night, and I'll help you clean up tomorrow."

Avery finally sat next to her, and for the next few minutes, they ate in silence.

"I was thinking that we could do the Christmas tree together...next weekend maybe? We might not be here the whole time, but it's nice to come back to, don't you think?"

And where would they be? This was going to be a lot more complicated than spending the night. Clare had often mentioned that her parents, like Avery's, would like her to come back to her hometown. Like Avery, Clare loved her parents, but she also loved living and working in the big city. She'd still go home for Christmas?

"Yeah, that sounds nice."

At her apartment, Avery and her roommates put up a small tree every year, usually with funky decorations. Judging from the decorations already in place, she could tell that Clare's taste was a bit more luxurious. Her apartment was cozy, but she had to make a comfortable living to be able to live here by herself.

Avery's thoughts drifted as she remembered a short freelance gig she'd been lucky to land with Jay & Parker, before she'd even met Clare. They paid well, but it was hard to get a foot in the door.

"Let's do it, then." Clare yawned. "I'm afraid I'll be out for the count soon."

"I can sleep out here," Avery offered. "You should get some rest."

"You're not serious, are you?"

"Yes, I am. You might not remember, but I toss and turn. And I'll check on you every few hours anyway, remember?"

"Yes, sure, but why can't you sleep in the bed? That is...weird. Are you sure we didn't have a fight?"

"No, it's not that." Avery wished she could tell her she wanted nothing more than sleep next to her and hold her close. At the moment, even the thought seemed inappropriate. "Just for tonight, okay?"

Clare shrugged. Avery could tell she wasn't convinced. She couldn't blame her.

Chapter Five

CLARE

Clare was still taken aback by Avery's insistence to sleep on the couch, but she was too tired to worry about it much. Before turning off the lights, she checked her phone, reassured to find no urgent messages. She scrolled a bit further to find a photo of the two of them holding huge mugs with hot chocolate, both of them smiling widely. Avery was wearing...an elf costume?

She couldn't access the complete memory, only fragments of it, but they were all comforting. Avery's laughter, the taste of the hot chocolate, Christmas music playing, and wonder in the eyes of small children.

Clare turned off the light and closed her eyes, smiling in the dark. She'd ask Avery about the costume tomorrow. A few hours of sleep would make all the difference in the world.

She slipped into a deep sleep, those impressions woven into her dreams, until a gentle touch to her arm woke her.

"I'm sorry," Avery whispered, looking the part. "How are you?"

Clare couldn't hold in the yawn. "Fine. Tired. I'm sorry, I know it's not your fault. Come here for a moment?"

Avery brushed her hand over Clare's arm, but she didn't budge.

"How's the headache? Any other symptoms?"

"I'm good. No headache." Aware of the hint of impatience in her tone, she relented. "Don't worry. And thank you so much for being here."

"Of course," Avery said quietly. "I'll see you in a few hours."

Falling back asleep was surprisingly easy, given the many questions on her mind. Clare consoled herself with the fact that Avery was steadfast by her side. They could figure out the rest later.

Her sleep was interrupted two more times. When she woke by herself in the morning, the apartment was quiet. Checking the clock on the nightstand, Clare realized she still had about half an hour before she would have to get up to get to work in time. Perhaps she could manage to go in a little later. That should be an acceptable compromise for her bosses, especially if she mentioned the concussion.

She frowned, still not recalling how she'd ended up losing her footing on the sidewalk. Or leaving work. Or the workday. The married couple that ran the agency was nothing but generous and appreciative of their employees, but in the past year, she'd never seen anyone have alcohol on the job. She couldn't imagine she had ever initiated such a thing. That left bad luck.

She got up and stealthily snuck into the living room where Avery looked quite comfortable on the couch. Clare felt instantly guilty, realizing she hadn't even offered sheets and extra pillows. Fortunately, Avery knew her way around...Why wouldn't she? They'd just celebrated an anniversary.

She smiled, feeling triumph at the returning memory. A tiny candle in a pastry. Avery looking so happy. She bent down, wincing at the strain in her back, but carried on with her plan and placed a soft kiss on Avery's cheek.

"Good morning, Christmas elf," she whispered. It would be okay. Things were falling into place, details were coming back to her...

She had to react fast and step back when Avery bolted upright, looking disoriented.

"Clare! Are you all right?"

"I should ask you that. Did you have a nightmare?"

Avery looked around as if she saw the apartment for the first time and pulled the blanket up higher.

"I don't think so. I'm sorry."

"Don't worry. We still have time...Wait, did you sleep in your clothes?"

"You were asleep so fast. I didn't want to wake you."

Clare didn't know what to do other than shake her head at the absurdity of the situation.

"Come on, you could have just taken anything. I must have been a bad girlfriend if you thought I'd be particular about it." Her joke seemed to be falling flat, so she decided to change the subject. "It's early though. We could stop by your place on the way to work?"

"Work...I mean, you're not going in for sure, and I thought I'd ask a co-worker to cover my shift. I'm sure he'll do it, except if I call him right now. He likes to sleep in..." Avery turned bright red and then added, "I don't know if you remember, but Max is my roommate too. I don't know all the sleeping habits of my co-workers. Anyway. There's no hurry. I'll be here as long as you need me."

"That is very kind of you, but I have to be in the office. All the doctor said was to take it easy."

"Exactly. That's why she told you to take a couple of days."

Clare suppressed a sigh. "Really? Honey, you know how important that project is. I would have to update someone, and frankly, I don't know if I'm ready to share the credit. I worked hard on this."

"I know. And I understand you're disappointed, but two days will go by quickly. I promise. Wait…" Avery looked confused all of a sudden. "Christmas elf? Why did you say that?"

"Are you testing me or something?" Much as she'd tried to hide it, her impatience shone through. "I have the picture. I do remember us being there."

"Okay. Good. I'm sorry." Avery raked a hand through her adorably disheveled hair. "It surprised me, that's all. What if I made us coffee, and we go from there?"

Clare couldn't stay irritated with her to save her life.

"Let's do that. I'll get dressed meanwhile, and I can lend you something. I don't want an argument. Remember I'm the pitiful, injured party."

"Injured yes. Pitiful? Far from it," Avery mumbled, making her laugh.

"I will call into work and gauge the situation. I won't be careless. I promise. I have so many plans for us this season."

"All right. You go ahead."

·♥·♥·♥·♥·♥·

She could get used to this. When Clare came out of the shower this time, Avery had breakfast on the table, the scent of coffee enticing. She paused before sitting down. Was she used to this? Had she immersed herself in her work so much that Avery was doing everything at home? She didn't know, and it bothered her. But Avery had said they didn't live together yet, so these were special circumstances. Clare didn't feel injured save for the occasional twinges reminding her of her encounter with the cold concrete.

She couldn't forget about it either because she kept hitting walls.

"I understand it must be frustrating." Setting a cup of coffee in front of her, Avery was reading her mind as usual. Her tone was soft, affectionate rather than patronizing.

"It is. I don't want to talk about it. Let's see how we best get through the next couple of days, and then do something special on the weekend, okay?" Her phone rang. "That can't be work already? I guess news travels fast," she mused before picking up.

"Clare, hi, this is Jay Diaz. I was told there was an incident yesterday. Are you okay?"

Why couldn't people mind their own business? She had almost expected that someone at work would have been happy to tell the bosses first.

"I'm fine." After receiving a pointed gaze from Avery, she elaborated. "The doctor said I have a mild concussion and should take it easy for a couple of days. I could come in…"

"No, you stay where you are and get some rest," he insisted. "If we need anything, we'll call you, I promise, but I think we'll be fine. You did meticulous work."

"Thank you. I'd prefer if I could continue to do that."

"I'll see you in a couple of days."

"I could come in later—"

"A couple of days means, two days. Get some rest."

"All right, boss. Thank you." She had barely clicked to end the call when it rang again. "I seem to be popular this morning. Hi, Mom."

"Clare, sweetie, I was taking a chance that you'd still be home. Have you thought about it?"

"Thought about what?"

"Are you doing this on purpose? That's not nice. What should I tell Eliza?"

"Who's Eliza?" She noticed Avery sit up straighter.

"I hope this really just slipped your mind. I told you about her yesterday. Your nephew's new teacher, Eliza Camden? I'd like to invite her to Christmas dinner. She's really looking forward to meeting you. You're not seeing anyone, right? You could give it a chance."

Maybe it was just as well that she couldn't work. It seemed like she had important matters to clear up. Had she not told them about Avery? That was impossible. Clare was certain that the moment they got together, she had shouted it from the rooftops. She cast a soft smile at Avery who was sipping her coffee, looking lost in thought.

"Mom, that might be a little awkward. Forgive me if I forgot mentioning it because..." At the last moment, she decided not to make too many revelations. Her family would worry unnecessarily. Worse, they might even use her accident as a reason why she needed to come home—regardless of how many people slipped on ice in Havenwood. "I'm going to bring Avery."

"Avery."

"My girlfriend."

The pause lasted for several seconds, until realization set in that both of them might have neglected to provide essential information. She cast a quick look at Avery, who was paying attention now, tense for some reason.

There had to be a lot more she wasn't telling her. Clare frowned. Her family wasn't homophobic—why would she have kept her relationship from them? Had Avery asked her to? Was going home for the holidays an issue? Had they fought over the possible mystery guest Eliza?

"Avery. That cute girl from the coffee shop you've been go-ing on about?" her mother finally asked. "Why didn't you say anything?"

That solved at least one problem.

"I'm sorry. We've both been busy."

"Well, we'll figure it out. That's great news, honey! We'd love to meet her. Is there a chance she's moving to Havenwood with you?"

Clare couldn't hold back the laughter.

"I don't think so, but nice try, Mom. Hang on a second." She switched to video chat. "You can say hello right now. Avery, my mom." She held the phone to Avery who waved with a hesitant smile.

"Hi, Mrs. Hartley."

"Avery. It's good to finally put a face to your name. We'll see you at Christmas, right?"

Seeing that she seemed uncomfortable, Clare decided this was enough of an introduction for now.

"We'll be there, Mom. You and Dad will still come by for your holiday shopping?"

"Not just for that," her mother scolded gently. "You know we have stores in Havenwood? But yes, we'll be in town next week for dinner. Then we can discuss Christmas some more...and Avery, you must come visit. Have Clare show you pictures, it's very beautiful at this time of year."

"Okay, Mom, I'll see you next week." Ending the call, she couldn't help noticing Avery's deer-in-the-headlights expres-sion. "I hope I didn't put you on the spot."

"You kind of did, but it's all right. Your mom is nice. And you remembered about the holiday shopping."

"Yeah, they do it every year, since long before I moved to the city. You're sure you'll be all right?"

"Yes. You?"

"Perfect. Some things are still a bit...nebulous. I must have kept you to myself for quite some time...but I was so relieved when you were the first person I saw. For a moment I wasn't sure of anything, except that I know you, and I'm in love with you."

"I'm so sorry you had to go through this. I'm happy to be here for you."

Clare reached out to take her hand. "You are doing a great job. And now that we're basically having a snow day, what are we going to do with it? Do you want to go back to bed?"

Chapter Six

AVERY

C lare was starting to sense that something was up. How could she not when Avery was stumbling through every situation that should be normal for a couple? She had to tell her at some point. There was no way she could meet the parents for dinner, let alone spend Christmas with the family.

Why did having to give that up feel like someone was tearing her heart out? Avery didn't have to look hard. This was everything she had dreamed about for almost a year. A fantasy. Now it was all in reach, but if she went along with everything, that would make her a horrible person. Taking advantage of Clare's situation was the last thing she wanted.

But she was so happy, so secure in her belief that the two of them were together. Did that mean she had wanted them to? What was wrong with the both of them being happy?

Should she go back to meet with Dr. Mason?

It had been a bit scary, having to wake Clare and worrying that her symptoms might have gotten worse. Thank the

Universe, that hadn't been the case. Avery's thoughts wandered back to the first time she'd gone into Clare's room, watching her sleep for an entire minute or so like a creep—because she didn't want to startle her. By the third time, she'd been doing better, and Clare didn't ask any more questions because all she wanted was to go back to sleep. But now she was awake and aware, and Avery had a multitude of other things to worry about.

Still marveling at the fact that she was here in Clare's kitchen, like she belonged, like they were really a couple. Therein lay her dilemma.

"Since you still haven't answered my question, I assume the answer is no to going back to bed?"

"I'm sorry. You need some more rest. I have to call Max and ask him about my shift."

"I know. I was joking." Clare was still holding her hand, making Avery nervous. At the same time, she craved the tender, innocent contact—except it wasn't all that innocent if Clare believed…The heat rushed to her face again. That would happen a lot more in the near future, unless Clare's memory returned soon.

"I have to take a look at my files too, maybe make a couple of calls. In the meantime…"

"I'll take care of mine," Avery agreed, feeling bereft when Clare withdrew her hand. "Don't worry. I'll make sure you take it easy and don't get bored."

She could handle difficult customers with a smile day in, day out. She could handle this…falling in love with Clare Hartley even more.

·♥·♥·♥·♥·♥·

To Avery's relief, Max picked up right away, and as she'd hoped, he had no problem covering for her.

"Thank you!" she exclaimed. "You're a lifesaver."

"Can I ask what that emergency is?" he asked, sounding concerned. "Are you okay?"

That was yet to be determined. Avery didn't want to give him the wrong impression.

"I'm fine, just helping out a friend." She lowered her voice even though Clare was still in her bedroom. Avery cast a look at the closed door. What was she going to tell Clare tonight? Redirecting her focus to the matter at hand, she continued, "I'll explain later. I'll probably be back sometime tomorrow."

"Okay. Take good care of yourself...and your friend...and let me know if you need anything."

"I will. Thank you so much."

That had been easy. Now, regarding her promise. Avery stepped to the window, realizing that a substantial amount of snow had fallen in the past few hours. Not a bad time to stay in.

She went to the TV, checked a few channels, and favorited a few choices. Then she checked the kitchen again. Avery couldn't help feeling like she was snooping, but it was important that she did everything right in the next couple of days. If she could be the perfect girlfriend as long as Clare needed her to be, maybe she would forgive her if she found out that they had never been together.

That, too, might be nothing but a fantasy, but Avery was willing to give it her best.

· ♥ · ♥ · ♥ ·

What to do on a snowy day when you couldn't go out? It might not be a coincidence that Avery got a gig as Christmas elf every year since she had moved to the city. Her task was to take pictures of the kids with Santa, and she had enjoyed every moment of it.

Last year, even more so when Clare came by, blinking before she recognized the barista from *The Ground Floor*. Avery had never told her that her name actually meant Christmas elf. Now she had to go above and beyond the job. Not that it was a job, but a strange alternate universe she'd slipped into. No, a lie.

The doctor hadn't asked her to lie, just not to push. How could she do one without the other?

Regardless, when Clare came out of her bedroom, she had the first phase of entertainment ready. One step at a time.

"Since we don't have to go out today, I checked the selection, and there are a few cute movies. Some on demand, and I programmed a few."

"Uh...That is nice."

Avery hadn't realized until now that Clare was carrying her purse.

"I thought your bosses agreed that you should stay home."

"Yes, in theory...but I need to go in for a few minutes. Can't you come with me? I haven't had a headache, nausea, or dizziness. So, I lost a day, but I have to get over that. It might never come back."

"I don't know." If she failed to keep Clare resting at home for a day, how could she justify keeping up the lie? Avery cringed. She didn't want to call it that. Even arguing with Clare here in her apartment seemed oddly more comforting than her dreams. In any case, she couldn't leave her alone.

"It will be less than an hour in and out, I swear," Clare promised. "We could get groceries on the way home and cook something nice, and of course we'll still watch all the movies." She stopped herself, frowning. "This is something we do, right?"

"Yes." Sort of. A few mornings last year, they had talked about the movies they'd watched, laughing together about all the overly sweet happy endings, the copious amounts of hot chocolate consumed, and the tropes they both enjoyed. She'd only known Clare for a short time, but somehow Avery had already dreamed of a happy ending like that. The friendship they had formed seemed more realistic, but at the same time, bittersweet. "Okay. But promise me, you won't take long. I could catch up with Max in the meantime."

"Perfect. Thank you. I hope your boss is not giving you a hard time for taking a couple of days of in the midst of the season."

"No, it's okay," Avery mumbled. "Let's do this."

"Don't worry. I'll be fine."

CLARE

Clare hadn't lied—entirely. She still felt shaken by the experience, more emotionally than physically. On the bright side—Avery. She kept telling herself that it could have been so much worse. She could have forgotten all about her life before the incident, the job, worse, people she loved, but that wasn't the case.

The grey spots in her memory still bothered her, because sometimes it felt like they went beyond that one day, that small details had been swept up in them.

She was tired too but certain that checking in with her colleagues would help.

Avery had insisted on taking a cab which took longer than the subway would have, but Clare didn't argue. She was simply grateful to be with her.

The advantage of a slow cab ride was having another point of view on the decorations. Excitement won over her weariness as she imagined the many activities the city offered around the season. She and Avery would have the best time ever.

She considered it necessary to consult with colleagues during her absence, but she wasn't a hopeless workaholic. She would take time for the things that mattered most, and when her parents came to visit, they would hopefully see that she belonged here.

"I won't be long. I promise," she said again when they parted ways in front of *The Ground Floor*. When she leaned in for a kiss, Avery hesitated. For all her eagerness to help, the way she acted did feel confusing to Clare, like she was still missing something. Was Avery not out at work?

That was near impossible. Jay & Parker were a married couple, and everyone knew it. Why would there be a different set of rules for the coffee shop?

She watched as Avery went aside and headed to the counter, then turned to the elevator and went up to her floor.

She hadn't made it all the way to her desk when Parker Hall came her way.

"Hartley, what are you doing here? I hope it's to pick up your invitation for the Christmas party? Jay told me what happened. Are you okay?"

"Fine, thank you. I'm not even here, officially. I just wanted to make sure everyone has what they need."

"That's better. Get out of here as soon as you can," he advised. "The circumstances might not be the best, but you've earned it."

"I'll be back the day after tomorrow. Avery and I have a lot of plans this season."

Clare nearly sighed in relief when he didn't blink. Finally, someone who was aware of their relationship. "Anyway, I'll check in with the team, and go home after that."

"You do that. And thank you."

"You're welcome."

Avery had a point, she realized about a half hour later when she took the elevator back down. Everyone had been happy to see her and assured her they could handle any storm that might come their way for a couple of days. She had taken the envelope that contained the fancy invitation to the party, from her desk.

Clare didn't feel like sitting down and doing another ten-to-twelve-hour day. Having to take a sick day during the season was no fun, but perhaps that was the universe's way of telling her to halt for a moment?

Maybe she hadn't valued everything good in her life outside of work enough. It was hard to do when she'd been trying to make a name for herself, and a home in the city.

A home. Her thoughts and emotions were still all over the place. Maybe this Christmas, she could ask Avery to move in. So many questions she still needed to ask Avery. Lucky for her, the woman she had fallen in love with seemed to have endless patience.

Chapter Seven

AVERY

"You finally asked her out? The girl you said was far out of your league? That was your emergency? Wow, way to go, Avery!"

Max sounded both incredulous and admiring. Avery had more reason to cringe, her face burning as she sat at the counter, nursing the cappuccino Max had prepared for her. She didn't feel like she deserved his enthusiasm or support, but she did remember mentioning Clare in these terms. She had always been more than a crush, but out of reach, unthinkable that they could be more than casual friends. They hadn't even hung out together.

She was in big trouble.

"She's a grown woman. Aside from that—did you not listen to me? She fell and was out for a moment. I went to the hospital with her, and because she had a concussion, she needed someone to stay with her."

"I get that part. Even checking in at work. That doesn't explain the kissing part."

"It's complicated," she admitted.

"Why? You've been pining for her for so long...Why aren't you happier?"

"I am. I'm sorry, that was a huge scare."

"I understand, but you just can't keep something like this from me."

"I guess you're right. Don't tell anyone yet, please?"

What was she doing?

"My lips are sealed," he promised.

Avery was sure he had more questions, and she would deal with them once she was back home. Speaking of which, she had to get a change of clothes. There was no way she could take up Clare on her offer.

·♥·♥·♥·♥·♥·

Clare seemed in good spirits when she returned from her floor, and Avery was more than ready to go. To be home with her pretend girlfriend was one thing, out in the world, something entirely different.

She had to tell her. Today. Clare was a smart accomplished woman. She wouldn't fall off a cliff when she learned the truth, just be...disappointed? Angry? Avery resented Dr. Mason, even though she knew the doctor wasn't solely responsible for putting her in this position. Avery had contributed, more than her share, because she'd wanted this so much.

Focus on the practical, she reminded herself. Get some groceries, get Clare home safely—she guessed it would be okay to leave her alone for a bit to get a few clothes. In the evening, if she still wasn't showing any adverse symptoms...They'd have to have that conversation.

They had decided to walk to the grocery store and take a cab from there, but when they walked past the stalls of the Christmas market on Alcott Square, Clare stopped her.

"What is it? Am I walking to fast?"

"No." Clare laughed. "I didn't hurt my leg. I was just thinking...We'll come back in the evening another time, but how about we go take a first look? I'll tell you if I'm tired."

To her surprise, Avery didn't object at all.

"I can go to the store by myself," she offered.

"We'll see. I want to walk around a bit and look for potential Christmas gifts. I don't know how I always end up doing it last minute—so maybe this is a sign."

"Maybe it is," Avery agreed.

CLARE

Clare linked her arm with Avery's, and they explored the various vendors' offerings, from arts and crafts to all kinds of sweet and savory delicacies. Strange how she didn't even feel guilty for not being at her desk. Only a few people, mostly tourists, were browsing the stalls at the moment. The music was playing softly in the background, and the sights and scents around her were deeply comforting. They walked past the space where Santa's workshop had already been put up. Santa and the elves would arrive next week. This was where she and Avery had taken the selfie last year.

"You're going to put on that costume again soon," she said with a smile.

"I will. It's not exactly the stellar career you have, but it's a gig, and it's always fun."

They walked a few steps in silence. Her optimism and ability to turn a challenging situation around was one of the things Clare loved most about Avery. Clare had come to the city for that one chance, and she wouldn't know what to do if she hadn't landed the job with Jay & Parker.

Avery had come to document the world through her eyes, and she was working on the Christmas market and occasionally, weddings and other events. Her photography was mostly displayed in the coffee shop where she worked full-time as a barista.

Clare lost her train of thought when they came to stand in front of a display of snow globes. She admired all of them, especially the one that had tiny figurines ice-skating around the huge Christmas tree.

Avery, as usual, had noticed. Clare continued to walk when she turned around and realized Avery had fallen behind, only now catching up to her. With a hopeful smile, she held up the bag.

"You noticed."

"Of course. You told me you had one like this as a kid."

"Do you ever forget a thing?" Clare hoped that her tone was even enough to take any possible sting out of her words. She didn't mean to bring everything back to the unfortunate incident. "You didn't have to do this."

"It's an early Christmas present."

"Well, in that case, thank you." She leaned in to kiss her, and this time, Avery kissed her back. "I swear, I'm almost ready to go, but we finish this with a hot chocolate?"

"You're lucky I can't say no to you." Avery had a dreamy expression on her face.

"I'm lucky. That's all I need to know."

Chapter Eight

AVERY

She had so much to make up for, Avery didn't even know where to start. But start, she would, right this evening. She had packed a change of clothes just in case, though she doubted Clare would want to see her again after the revelations.

Avery blinked back tears as she walked along the aisles of the supermarket. Maybe it wouldn't be so bad. Maybe a snow globe connected to a childhood memory, and a homecooked meal made with love would make a difference...*right*.

She'd always have that kiss, Clare's lips soft and warm on hers, music playing in the background...Avery couldn't resist. She would always carry that memory with her. The best Christmas. It still had potential to become the saddest Christmas, but she'd carry on as always. Find a new job maybe since Clare wasn't going anywhere. She had a bright future at Jay & Parker's. Perhaps it had been a sign, too, when they didn't offer Avery a permanent position after her short stint with them.

As she put item after item into the cart, Avery hoped Clare would give her a chance to explain. She enjoyed working at *The Ground Floor*, interacting with customers, remembering the beverage that put a smile on their faces and made their days a little brighter...The way she'd felt when Clare first walked into the coffee shop was in a different dimension. She had been drawn to her right away.

Even though she'd sensed that Clare might not be this open with every stranger, she found her easy to talk to, someone she had no reservations sharing her dream with. Soon she had started dreaming of sharing a lot more than that with her...But Avery and her dreams didn't matter.

The doctor had warned about forcing the memory to come back. Avery was no expert, and she didn't believe in researching health conditions online. It made sense to her that you didn't submit someone who was already hurt to more stress.

That, and Clare had been so insistent, obviously happy with what she believed to be a fact...Happy. Avery couldn't stop smiling, even knowing that her giddiness would come to an end soon. Clare remembered her right away, and she was happy thinking they were together.

She needed a moment, a few minutes to herself to wonder what that could mean.

Then she had to hurry up, because tonight's dinner would be made with all fresh ingredients, from appetizer to desserts.

·♥·♥·♥·♥·♥·

She returned to the apartment, carrying full grocery bags and her overnight bag. "I think we have everything we need."

Clare had turned on the Christmas lights around the house again, and curiously gazed into each bag. "I wish we could have a glass of wine with that, but the doctor said to wait a few days. What are we cooking?"

"You've had enough moving around for today. I can handle this."

"I can chop something."

Truth be told, given her plans for tonight, Avery was sure having Clare watch her would make her more nervous. Again, she couldn't find it in her to refuse.

What a lousy Christmas elf she turned out to be.

"Why are you so nervous? I'm fine. I'll just do a few hours at work this week, no heavy lifting. I am not careless, you know. I want us to have the best holidays ever."

"I want that too."

When Clare stood behind her and wrapped her into a hug, Avery couldn't help leaning into her. It felt too familiar, too right. Maybe *she* had taken a hit to the head and was imagining all of this? In that case, the guilt that plagued her was entirely unfair. Either way, her subconscious seemed to work much different from Clare's.

"Okay, you can sit and chop a few veggies. I'll do the rest."

"Whatever you like." Clare placed a soft kiss on her neck that sent a pleasant shiver down her spine. She went to pour two glasses of water and handed one to Avery. "Let's start with this."

Focusing on the meal, Avery started by preparing the chicken breasts she cooked with vegetables and rice. The egg rolls went into the oven. While the chicken was cooking, she made the dessert, a quick chocolate orange mousse that would cool and set in the fridge while they were having dinner.

As usual, busying herself with practical issues helped clear her mind. She hadn't done anything horrible, or at least not with evil intent.

Clare would believe her. She had to. And they could go back to being friends...Avery suppressed a sigh. She didn't know what was worse.

Clare being mad at her or wanting to go back to the way things were before.

·♥·♥·♥·♥·♥·

During the meal, she tried to be stealthy and observe Clare. Avery was failing on the stealthy part.

"Everything is perfect, don't worry," she assured Avery, a hint of amusement in her tone. "See? I haven't lost my appetite. You know it takes a lot for that to happen...In fact, I don't even think you've experienced that yet."

That was actually true. Clare often came to *The Ground Floor* hungry. Her coffee choices varied, but she ordered a pastry or a sandwich most of the time. That cinnamon bun...It seemed like forever ago. Before they had kissed. Before dinners in romantic lighting.

"Since tomorrow is a real day off, how about we clean up in the morning?" Clare suggested. "We could do a couple of movies tonight."

On a whim, Avery decided that after those movies, it would still be early enough to come clean. If she was lucky, they would put Clare in a forgiving mood?

"Sounds great."

After dinner, they rinsed the dishes and left them in the sink. With their dessert, they retreated to the softly lit living room.

Clare sighed in bliss. "I have to say this is the best sick day I've ever had. An early Christmas present, I get to spend all day with you, you're cooking for me, and now we're going to watch cheesy movies. I'm in heaven already."

"I'm glad you like desserts," Avery blurted out, prompting Clare to laugh. She reached out to brush her fingers over Avery's cheek, something she seemed to be fond of doing. Avery couldn't complain either. "Let's just...watch that movie, okay?"

It was alarmingly easy to forget about the reason why she was here, just allow herself to get lost in the warmth of the moment. Avery suppressed a yawn, and halfway through the movie, she realized that Clare was nodding off too.

"You should go to bed. We can finish them tomorrow, too."

"Just this one. I want to know how it ends."

"I don't want to spoil you, but...the way they all end. I'm pretty sure."

"Just a few more minutes." Clare picked up a comforter from the armrest of the couch and pulled it over the two of them.

Yeah, just a few more minutes...

Avery tried to focus on the story unfolding on the screen, but her mind was a whole lot more occupied with real life.

Despite her insistence, Clare was gravitating towards her, almost asleep. She cuddled up to Avery who had never said the words she'd planned to say.

"I'm so glad you are here," Clare whispered. "I won't lie to you, that was kind of scary."

"I know. It scared me too."

It had, though now that she knew Clare would be all right, something else scared Avery.

"There's something we need to talk about."

Clare's response was to snuggle closer to her.

"I know I made you uncomfortable this morning. I'm sorry. I swear, everyone in my family is quite nice, even if they won't stop asking me to come home."

"That's not it. About your memory..."

"I don't want to talk about it," Clare said, her tone final. "Avery, I have a lot on my mind, and I still want to enjoy the holidays, with my family, most of all, with you..."

Clearly, Avery had failed to keep her conflicting emotions out of her expression because Clare paused to ask, "Are you okay?"

"Yes. Of course." What else was she going to say?

"Are we in any huge legal or financial trouble that I don't know about? Or both?"

"Not that I know of. Why?"

"Easy," Clare returned. "Everything else, I really don't want to know about at the moment. My memory...it's just one day. It's not important."

Avery was about to give it one last try and protest, but words failed her when Clare sank her hand into her hair.

"You are."

"Okay," Avery whispered. Did that mean she had permission to continue the illusion—one that served them both?

"Thank you. Now let's go to bed, and no sleeping on the couch or anything like that."

Breathing in the scent of Clare's perfume, Avery had neither the strength nor the will to object. For most of her life she had simply gone with the flow. It had provided her with a talent, a home, a job she enjoyed...And now, love. Who was she to mess with any of it?

Chapter Nine

CLARE

Despite the delicious dinner and spending time watching movies they both enjoyed, there had been tense moments throughout the evening. Clare wasn't oblivious. She knew that Avery might be stressed about meeting her parents, about being out to friends and family in general maybe. Clare wanted to make it as easy for her as possible. She felt incredibly relieved when Avery didn't insist on sleeping on the couch this time.

Strange, to think that their relationship might be relatively new, when it felt like they had known each other forever. Her memory was still vague on some details, and she didn't want to worry Avery. She might return to Dr. Mason's and ask her if this was normal.

At least, she could easily access all the specifics of the project, which would keep her working, and a roof over her head. It was disconcerting to think that she couldn't remember some of the details regarding her relationship with Avery, but she knew she loved her. She loved hearing her laugh, and she loved being close to her, like now.

Everything else would come together.

She knew it would.

Soon, it would be Christmas, after all.

·♥·♥·♥·♥·♥·

If there was any residual unease left, Clare didn't find it hard to push it aside. Waking Avery with a tender kiss, she knew she had to bring up the subject of moving in together soon.

It made so much sense—they worked out of the same building. Avery might even get another job with Jay & Parker in the future. And she loved looking into Avery's sleepy expression first thing in the morning.

"You can stay a little bit," she whispered. "I'll make us breakfast today."

That woke Avery for good.

"No, you shouldn't. If you give me a few minutes..."

"Avery. Come on. Slow down. There's no rush today. You've done so much already. I swear I can handle it."

"Okay. Thank you." Avery pulled the covers higher around her, and for a heartbeat, Clare regretted her promise. Like the doctor had told her, like everyone kept telling her, she had to be patient. Not only with herself, but also with Avery.

Clare could only imagine. If the roles were reversed, she'd likely be in shock, wanting to take things slow. Once Clare was back at work and they could resume their normal lives, it would be easier to convince Avery that she was and would be all right. She would take her out to dinner before they spent time with her parents.

In the kitchen, she prepared the coffee and set the table. The mild but noticeable vertigo came out of nowhere, with the fragment of a memory. Clare gripped the counter, both disturbed by the sensation and comforted by the vision of Avery talking to her after a confrontation with a difficult client.

"They hired you for a reason. I've worked with them before, and I'm sure they value your talent."

Clare took a deep breath, and, realizing that she had regained her balance, she went back to the task at hand, eggs, and bacon sizzling in a pan when Avery came to the kitchen.

"I hope this is okay."

"Of course. You didn't have to cook."

"Come on. Don't be such a bummer," the words came out before she could censor them. "You've been cheerleading me through some really difficult times. When that client yelled at me in front of everyone? Jay later apologized for them, but at that moment I thought I'd pack my bags and go right back to the family business."

"I remember that." Avery poured coffee for the two of them and put two slices of bread into the toaster. "I couldn't imagine Jay or Parker would let them treat you like that."

"Well, they didn't, which turned out to be a good thing. The company went bankrupt after being taken to court over fraud."

"Right. What do you want to do today?" Avery asked.

"If you're not bored senseless, I'll catch up on some work, and we could watch a couple more of those movies?"

"No. That's perfect."

Chapter Ten

AVERY

Their temporary arrangement had to come to an end. When she left for work the next morning after assuring herself that Clare was ready to tackle the day by herself, Avery was stunned by the sense of loss she felt.

She couldn't go on having Clare believe they were together, but in Clare's mind they were. After spending the night snuggled up to her, and a couple of days of Christmas activities, Avery's mind, too, had trouble letting go of the idea.

They fit together. They understood each other's tastes, dreams, and goals. They were comfortable in each other's company.

They were meant to be—except one coincidence, and one resulting mistake, might have ruined it all.

Clare didn't come to *The Ground Floor* this morning, since they'd had breakfast together.

Avery wished she could talk to Max, but he wasn't working today, and besides, what could she have told him? The truth?

If it made her cringe to think about what she had done, how would he react?

To her relief, she was soon busy creating specialty drinks for customers, with no time to worry about a potential upcoming catastrophe—or the anti-climactic ending of her fantasy love story.

She would have to give Clare an explanation. In her defense, she'd tried, and Clare had brushed her off, gently but firmly. What if she did remember and really didn't want to know? Would that mean they were even?

When Avery closed the shop in the evening, she was none the wiser. She didn't want to be "even." She wanted things to be simpler, but that didn't seem to be an option.

·♥·♥·♥·♥·♥·

Coming home to her own apartment felt both comforting and jarring, and she couldn't make up her mind which held the bigger part.

Max and Ryan were making dinner. Chantal and her girl-friend were playing a video game in the living room. After a short greeting, Avery went straight to her room.

What had she been thinking?

It had been too easy to pretend that the doctor's advice meant exactly that, playing along, withholding the truth from Clare, finding excuses to continue.

That didn't just put her on the Naughty List, it made her a terrible person. A terrible person who needed to move on already.

Clare had a lot to show for, to convince her parents she was where she should be. Her career was taking off.

Avery, one the other hand—living with three other people, one of them being her ex, was supposed to be a temporary arrangement. Three years later, she was still in the same apartment, with the same job. It was unlikely that Jay & Parker would hire her again if they hadn't done so in a year.

She'd been pining for the same woman without ever making a move, until that woman basically fell into her lap. The chance of a lifetime? A cruel twist of fate?

She didn't realize she was crying until she heard Max's concerned voice.

"Avery? What's wrong?"

Where to start?

·♥·♥·♥·♥·♥·

"You need to tell her," he stated in a tone that left no room for alternative avenues.

It wasn't exactly news to Avery.

"I know!" Lucky for her, dinner wasn't ready yet, and her friend was willing to listen without judgment. He did have advice for her though. Avery wasn't sure if she was ready to take it, even though she knew he was right.

"When are you going to do it?" he pressed. "Forget about it. Call her now."

"On the phone?" Her voice rose a notch. "No, I'm not going to do that. Maybe have a nice dinner somewhere private."

"You've already tried that," Max pointed out, shaking his head. "How did you even get here?"

A good question, Avery had to admit. Back in her familiar surroundings and life, it was hard to understand.

"I really like her." That sounded cringe-worthy, given what she had done. "I was so scared. And the doctor scared me too, even though I'm sure she didn't mean to. I felt like if I pushed Clare too hard, I might make things so much worse and..."

"And of course, you hoped it could be true," he said softly.

59

"Something like that."

"But she's better now, right, going back to work? She didn't have any symptoms aside from the memory loss, so perhaps now she could handle the truth?"

The real question was, could Avery?

"I suppose."

"You've been taking care of her. I'm sure she appreciates that, and maybe it's a good thing. She might give you another chance."

"Hey, guys, are you done in here?" Ryan peeked inside the room. "Dinner's ready."

Against all odds, Avery was hungry. The task ahead would take a lot of energy.

CLARE

She still hadn't told anyone in her family about the incident. When her brother called that evening, jokingly asking about her progress of getting into the holiday spirit, she slipped up.

"A sick day? What happened?"

She could basically hear him frown.

"Please, it's no big deal. I'm fine, Avery took care of me."

"Avery, the cute barista you keep talking about?"

To Clare's relief, he seemed to believe her. He didn't need to know about the memory loss.

"Yes, that's her."

"When are we going to meet her?"

"Soon, I promise. Meanwhile, please don't tell Mom and Dad. I don't want them to worry."

"Sure, if there's nothing to worry about."

They finished their conversation soon after, and Clare got ready for work. Almost as if nothing had happened.

After the short but disturbing detour, Clare felt like she was finally back on track—though walking past the patch where she had fallen still made her tense.

The rest...Couldn't have been better. Work kept her busy. It also kept her away from Avery, but they had been texting, and planned to have dinner on Saturday night.

Perhaps she could convince Avery, too, that she was doing fine? They could go back to the Christmas market at night. Maybe even get out of town on Sunday and take a sleigh ride? She loved the many opportunities that existed around the holidays, in the city, and just a few minutes' drive outside of it.

Avery would lose her hesitation. If Clare had any regrets, it was that she'd scared her this much, if not on purpose. She'd make it all up to her. Starting Saturday.

When Clare took out her wallet to pay for lunch she and her team had ordered, she realized that she was still carrying the invitation in her purse.

She was looking forward to taking Avery to Jay & Parker's prestigious Christmas party—because she was proud to have Avery by her side. At the same time, it might be a good time and place for her to form connections.

Clare knew better than anyone else how hard it was to get a foot in the door. If she could make things easier for Avery...It was something to put on her own Christmas wish list. For herself...She had the life she had always wanted, a loving family who, even though they would rather see her in Havenwood, somewhat grudgingly supported her ambitions. She got to share it all with a beautiful talented woman. What more could she ask for? There was perhaps one thing she could think of. Her face heated, and she quickly pushed the thought out of her mind when Parker Hall spoke to her.

"You're dreaming of the party? I don't blame you. It's going to be gorgeous."

"I have no doubt," she said, clearing her throat. "You remember Avery Murphy, right?"

"The photographer. Sure. We really liked her work, but we couldn't offer her another contract at the time."

He remembered her. That was a good sign.

"At the time, that means there would be an opening?"

"Not at this moment, I'm afraid. But she should submit again. You never know."

It wasn't quite the answer Clare had hoped for, but it was a start. She could work with that.

"True. Well, thanks for bearing with me these past few days. I swear I didn't plan to take time off in the midst of a new project."

"It's not your fault. You've been doing great work here. In fact, we're terrified that your parents might succeed in luring you back to the family business someday."

Now she was blushing for an entirely different reason.

"Thank you, Mr. Hall. I appreciate it."

"Since no one's looking, it's Parker," he said with a wink.

"Thanks. And about Avery..."

"Does she want to go to Havenwood?"

"No. I don't think so."

"Good. Please tell your parents Jay and I would like to make time for a meeting when they're in town."

"Sure."

A meeting? What else had she missed? She didn't dare ask. She couldn't imagine her parents would keep something like this from her, or that they would take their gentle meddling this far.

"Great. Have a good evening."

"You too, Mr. Ha—Parker."

She left the building, as usual careful to avoid that certain spot on the sidewalk, even though the ice had long been cleared away. As she walked along store windows decorated for Christmas, excitement won once more. There was snow in the forecast for the weekend, perfect for all the romantic activities she had on her mind.

She might be the opposite of a Grinch, but each Christmas still made her heart grow.

That was all she needed to remember.

·♥·♥·♥·♥·♥·

The restaurant they'd chosen was in walking distance of Clare's apartment, so Avery had come over with about an hour to spare until their dinner reservation.

"I'm so glad you're here," Clare said after a hug and a kiss that had both of them breathless. "You look amazing."

"You too." Avery was all but avoiding her gaze, almost shy. This was a side to her the customers of *The Ground Floor*, or the kids at Santa's workshop, didn't get to see. Clare felt like she might be overflowing with affection. Or that they might let that reservation expire and order in...She couldn't do that, could she? She had promised a romantic dinner.

"We still have some time. Would you like that we go have a drink at the bar, or here?"

"Maybe we leave now?" Avery suggested quickly. "It's not snowing yet."

"Okay." Clare noticed that Avery had only brought her purse, but they could address that later. She cherished the time they'd spend together relaxing and watching movies, but that had been sick leave. It was time to go back to their real lives. "Let's go. There are some amazing decorations in the neighborhood. We can take our time."

They were already in their coats when the doorbell rang.

"Are you expecting anyone?"

How was it possible that Avery sounded both relieved and anxious? Maybe she was right, and there was something they still had to talk about, especially before Christmas.

"No. Carolers maybe?"

A knock on the door followed. Frowning at the unexpected detour, Clare went to open and found herself enveloped in a tight hug the next moment.

"Surprise," her mother sing-songed.

Behind her, Clare's father smiled. "We thought we might come here a bit earlier and help you out. Christian and Shannon will bring the kids Monday, he's going to do the business part, and then we can all go out together."

"Doesn't that sound great?" her mother added.

Given how happy they were to have surprised her, and kind, to drop everything to get here early, she managed to keep the smile in place, and the slight disappointment out of her voice. Christian would hear from her though, for not keeping his mouth shut as she'd asked him to.

Behind her, Avery seemed frozen, until Diane Hartley spoke to her.

"And Avery, it's so nice to meet you in person. Thank you for taking such good care of Clare."

"Oh, I...I didn't do much."

"No, not much, only cook, clean, and keep me entertained and in good health. Mom, Dad, I'm glad you're here"—mostly—"but you don't have to do anything. I'm good, I'm back at work, and the doctor was satisfied with the latest tests."

"Well, that's great news then. We should go out and celebrate," Kevin Hartley suggested.

"That's...You're right. I'll call the restaurant and see if they can add another two to our table."

"Sounds great," he agreed.

Maybe this was a good thing after all. Avery would be meeting all of the family within the next few days, and that would put her at ease. Clare realized she still hadn't told her about the Christmas party at Jay & Parker's. No wonder people got scattered during the holidays, even when they loved the season...Time always seemed to move at record speed before it slowed down on Christmas Eve.

She gave Avery an encouraging look before she took her cell phone out of her purse to check with the restaurant.

Chapter Eleven

AVERY

This wasn't her fault, was it? Clare's parents showing up unexpectedly had not been in her plan. She didn't think they would appreciate her blurting out the truth over dinner. Besides, Avery needed time to explain to Clare, and she couldn't do that with her family around.

It had to wait. Max wouldn't be happy with her, but she had no choice.

Much as she would have loved a romantic dinner with Clare alone in this place, the presence of Diane and Kevin Hartley was a relief. She had sensed Clare's mixed emotions, but she, too, was enjoying herself when they sat at the bar with a cocktail, and her parents asked friendly nosy questions.

"You're a photographer, right?" Kevin Hartley said. "Have you ever thought about checking the market in Havenwood?"

"Dad," Clare scolded gently. "Could you be more obvious?"

"What? You said you're perfectly fine. So, we can go back to the second most important item on our agenda."

There was a hint of teasing in his voice that told Avery the family was used to this conversation, and while they would have loved Clare to come home, they understood that it wasn't going to happen anytime soon.

"Actually, these days I'm more a barista," Avery answered the question. "I do photo shoots for weddings and around the holidays."

"Yes." Clare had her phone in hand. "She's the cutest elf Santa has ever had the pleasure to work with," she explained, showing the picture to her parents.

Avery had many mixed emotions regarding the gesture. This picture had become some sort of anchor to the fantasy for Clare. Not that she could blame her. Avery hadn't done anything to help her correct it other than giving faint hints. Extremely faint hints.

"I can show you some of her other photographs later," Clare continued. "Oh, and if you meet with my bosses, you can check out *The Ground Floor*. Avery's been exhibiting her work there."

Avery hadn't missed the looks that passed between the couple.

"It's Christian who's going to meet with Jay & Parker," Diane said. "We're hiring them for a project. We couldn't really say anything earlier, because we didn't want to put you on the spot, but it looks promising..."

"Wait, what?"

Avery could easily tell from Clare's reaction that this was the first time she was hearing about said project.

"And if they decide to put you on it, that would be a good reason..." She held up her hands in mock defense. "Not going to say anything, I promise. There's no place like Havenwood in my opinion, but I can understand why you girls like the city." She gestured around the tastefully decorated bar.

"Give me a second here, Mom. Would that require whoever is on the project to work out of Havenwood?"

"Clare, Christian will figure out the details with them, and I promise he'll tell you everything," Kevin Hartley reassured her. "Now, there's something else we'd like to do while we are here. Your Mom has her eyes on some ornaments. We could do the shopping on Monday, before the kids arrive?"

"Maybe you'd like to stop at the Christmas market?" Avery suggested, hoping that sticking with a lighter subject might defuse the sudden tension. "You can find lots of beautiful gifts there."

Clare gave her a smile letting her know she'd seen through her, but she didn't object.

"Sounds great. Let's do it," Mr. Hartley decided. "We can take a first look on Monday and come back with everyone. You'll be joining us, right, Avery?"

"I can, Monday after work. I'll be on elf duty Tuesday afternoon, perhaps that would be interesting for the children?"

"Oh yes. My granddaughter claimed she's too old to see Santa, but she doesn't want to spoil it for her little brother," Diane explained, "...and I think she still believes a little."

"Don't we all?"

Avery noticed Clare's smile on her. It made her all warm inside. The cocktail might play a part too, but her feelings were real, had been for some time. Avery had a hard time seeing anything wrong with caring for someone, wanting them to be happy.

"That sounds like a plan. We could have dinner there."

"Yes, let's do that," Clare agreed. "And speaking of dinner, I think our table is ready."

⋅♥⋅♥⋅♥⋅♥⋅♥⋅

Warmth. Family. Love. Avery felt blessed with all of it, even though a small sliver of terror remained, for the moment when she might lose it all. At the moment, it barely registered.

It was already decided that she and Clare would spend Christmas Day at the Hartleys'. Avery usually left for her own parents' the day before Christmas Eve, and she might have suggested that this time, they'd go together and leave for Havenwood early in the morning. Max would not be pleased. She wouldn't be proud of herself in the morning, but tonight, she was basking in the comfort and joy of it all.

"I can't wait." Clare's eyes were sparkling in the light of the whimsical fixtures overhead. "See, we can have everything, enjoy spending time together here, and in Havenwood. I never said I'd never come back. I can't wait to show Avery."

Again, Clare's parents exchanged knowing gazes, making Avery wonder what they were thinking about. Yes, she was still dreaming of making it in the city, but if Clare changed her mind and asked her to move to Havenwood with her, Avery would say yes. Of course, she would.

She might have lost her mind.

·♥·♥·♥·♥·♥·

This time, she couldn't avoid wearing Clare's PJs. Avery quickly slipped under the covers after cleaning up in record time.

"Today was not quite what I had planned, but I loved it." Clare reached out to brush a hand over her hair, a guilty pleasure Avery couldn't resist. However, when Clare leaned over for a kiss that turned from soft and sweet to passionate in a heartbeat, she pulled back.

"I...I'm not really comfortable knowing your parents are next door."

"I know." Clare sighed as she lay back on her own pillow. "They usually take a hotel, but I guess they thought I needed more help. I told Christian not to tell them! I'm really sorry."

"Don't be. They're great. I'm happy to meet them."

"They're happy too." Clare's expression turned somber so quickly Avery felt like her heart had skipped a beat. Had she found out?

"Avery, you were right. We need to talk."

Now? When she had nowhere to go? She could already hear Max say, *told you so*. In her defense, there hadn't been any good moment...

"I guess you're right. I'm sorry."

"So you keep saying, but you never quite come out and tell me for what. Are you breaking up with me?"

Technically, that was where they were headed, except it was Clare who would likely do the breaking up once she knew the truth. Could you call it breaking up if everything had been an illusion to begin with?

"Avery, say something. Before the holidays? That is—"

"No!" She couldn't take it any longer, the hurt and disappointment in Clare's tone, after she'd been so happy all evening. They had been...they *were* happy. That part was real. Back to Plan A. "No, I'm not breaking up with you. I guess I'm still...I don't know. We've had a lot going on. I've never been as happy as I am with you."

Clare studied her for a long time.

"You know I feel the same way. Then why do you keep pulling away? I need you to be honest with me. If I did something to make you uncomfortable...I've been trying to remember, but I can't think of anything!"

"Oh no, it's not you. I promise." Hindsight was indeed 20/20, showing her all the ways she'd made things worse without thinking. Perhaps it was time to start with something else that was true. "You didn't do anything. We didn't..." Why was this so difficult? "I mean, we haven't...Not yet."

Clare looked puzzled for a few seconds until realization dawned.

"Oh...That's it?"

"I'm sorry," Avery tried again. To her surprise, Clare started laughing.

"I'm sorry, too. I'm not sure if that's the appropriate re-action." Her giggling was contagious. "Yeah, perhaps it's not funny I mixed that up, but it all makes sense now. I didn't mean to assume anything. Well, I did. You make me so happy in many ways, I couldn't imagine. Wow."

"I wasn't sure what to tell you and when," Avery admitted, a sense of relief filling her. "The doctor said not to force your memory, so..."

"You didn't say anything at all, and I was all over you."

"I kind of wanted you to..." She couldn't help it, initiating the kiss this time, though Avery stayed mindful of the fact that they weren't alone in the apartment.

"You're right," Clare agreed ruefully as she took her hand. "Let's wait until we have more privacy." She gave a tug, and Avery went eagerly into her arms. Problem solved...not.

Chapter Twelve

CLARE

Avery's hesitation never meant she wanted to end things—all it meant was that Clare had been getting ahead of herself. She could take a step back, take things slowly, especially when they both had so many dreams.

First: The holidays. Avery had fallen asleep before Clare could mention the Christmas party, and things had been a little rushed in the morning. Both Clare and Avery had gone to work, while her parents had taken off to explore the city on their own. They would meet them at *The Ground Floor* and go to the Christmas market from there.

When she made it downstairs that evening, she saw that Avery was still busy with a last customer. Her parents were sitting at a table by the window, waving when they saw Clare.

"She'll be done in a few minutes," her mother said. "We were just looking at her photographs. She is very talented."

Clare followed her gaze to the wall where Avery's work was displayed.

"Yes, she is."

"Perhaps there could be an opening at your firm sometime," her dad commented. He and her mother shared a knowing look, and predictably, he continued. "And if there isn't, well…"

"Mom, Dad, no. Can we please forget about this?"

"Okay, okay. It's too easy. But it's also easy to see that you're happy, here at your job, and with her. As long as you come home for the holidays…"

He didn't finish the sentence, as Avery had joined them at their table.

"Are you all ready? I'll just have to lock up, and we can go."

"I can't wait," Diane said, sounding excited. Clare was excited too. Things were going even better than she had hoped.

·♥·♥·♥·♥·♥·

At the market, they browsed the stands again. Clare couldn't help smiling when she remembered the time she and Avery had come here a few days ago.

Avery seemed to be thinking about it too, because when they walked past the stand with the snow globes, she whispered, "I'm so glad you're okay."

Clare laid an arm around her waist.

"More than okay, actually. And before I forget again, you'll be my plus one at the Christmas party, right? That's not a surprise," she added when Avery's eyes widened.

"No…I don't know. I didn't think about it. Thank you."

"Of course. It will be so much fun. Jay and Parker are far from Scrooges. Hm…Why didn't I take you last time?"

"We weren't together yet, but I was already in love with you."

If that was the case, why did she remember Avery wishing her a Happy Anniversary?

"Are you hungry?" Her parents, already carrying several bags, had caught up with them, and Clare got distracted from her questions. Who cared? Yummy food was in the near future.

"Starving!" she exclaimed. If her memory loss had taught her anything, it was that she wanted to spend as much time as possible with the people she loved. That, above all else, made sense to her.

Chapter Thirteen

AVERY

She did her best to avoid Max the next day. He wouldn't prod, but she couldn't keep the truth from him forever. Avery preferred to stay in her temporary sweet bubble where she was welcomed into the family and would accompany Clare to the prestigious party at Jay & Parker. She might even make connections...

Though, if she was honest, any possible career opportunities were far from her mind at the moment.

Avery kept going back to what Clare told her, about her fears to be dumped before Christmas. That was the worst trope of all. She didn't want to hurt Clare, just the opposite. Knowing how much she loved the holidays, those words had hit home with Avery, not that she had come up with any brilliant idea on how to solve her dilemma.

As she changed into Avery the Christmas elf in a backroom behind Santa's workshop, she could hear the voices of excited children. For a moment she remembered her own excitement at that age. She could imagine Clare...Okay, that might be weird. But adult Clare still loved Christmas so much, the comfort part, the family part, the glitz and glitter of the big city...love.

Wouldn't it be cruel to withhold it if Avery could give her all of that?

She might be getting megalomaniacal, but after watching Clare carefully, since her accident and before, Avery had learned a few things about her so-called girlfriend, and about herself.

They could have it all together. Why destroy something beautiful? The problem was she would have to lie to her for the rest of their lives, and sow doubt about Clare's memory even when she got it right. No, that wasn't true either. Just about the past year, and how they got together.

Could a lifetime of love make up for a lie this big?

Part of Avery was scared beyond measure, wanting to curl up in a corner and cry. She knew the answer, had always known it.

A knock on the door jolted her out of her dire musings. Santa, a student from the local university earning a few extra bucks, opened the door.

"Ready to rock?"

She couldn't help laughing at his delivery.

"You bet. Let's spread some holiday cheer."

·•·♥·♥·♥·♥·

For the next couple of hours, Avery had no time to dwell as she took picture after picture of children excited to see Santa. The latter had changed every year she'd had this assignment, and this one seemed especially in his element, even though she assumed him to be younger than her.

When he took a break, she did too, finding Clare and her parents in the crowd with Clare's brother, his wife, and their two kids. The older one, a girl, gave her a skeptical look as if she didn't believe Avery was for real.

Suppressing a sigh, she said, "Hi! Anyone of you want to see Santa after the break?"

"Yes!" The boy jumped up and down.

"Okay, maybe," the girl acknowledged.

"So that's settled." Clare laughed. "Avery, this is my niece Sara, and Sam, my nephew. My brother Christian, and my sister-in-law Shannon. Everyone, my magical elf girlfriend Avery."

"It's so lovely to meet you all. I'm afraid Clare might be exaggerating on the magic."

"Oh, I'm not. You're coming to dinner with us today, right?"

"Clare told us a lot about you," Clare's brother Christian said. "It's on us. We have something to celebrate."

"Right," Clare replied. "I can't believe you hired my agency. Mom and Dad will really try every angle."

"I swear I'm innocent in this. I was just told to negotiate the best deal," he joked. "Seriously, it would be good to have you home, but this was a great opportunity for us either way. So, now that we're here, what do you recommend?"

"Around here? Only everything. Wait until you've tasted the mulled wine. You will understand why I'm not going back to Havenwood."

Clare, like her brother, kept her tone light.

"We have lovely Christmas markets too," Diane Hartley commented, making everyone laugh.

"I have another hour or so," Avery said, looking behind her to see that Santa was waving at her.

"Great. We'll be back to pick you up."

She and Clare parted with a hug and a kiss, and she headed back to Santa's workshop where another line had formed.

"So, she took it well?"

Avery spun around, her heart in her throat when she saw Max. Fortunately, Clare and her family had already moved on.

"Could you keep it down?"

"I can't believe this," he said, his disapproval showing in his expression. "You still haven't told her?"

"I can't, not now. Besides, I'm working."

"Avery. I'm not trying to be mean. This isn't going to end well."

The look Clare's niece had given her popped into Avery's mind.

"I know. But it will be Christmas soon, and Clare loves Christmas. Like, really loves it. I can't ruin it for her."

"A lot more than Christmas will be ruined if you don't come clean," he predicted.

"You're right. I can't argue with any of it. And yet..."

Max shook his head. "Avery, it's not going to be better after the holidays. What happened to trying to explain? You were scared, you misunderstood the doctor...She might get that. The longer you drag it out, the harder it will be on both of you."

"I'm in love with her," Avery whispered, unsure if he had even heard her.

"Avery, you coming?" Santa called, and Avery didn't wait for Max to react. Saying it out loud might matter, but it didn't change the facts.

She couldn't evade the truth much longer. The question was whether she'd still buy a dress for that party.

·♥·♥·♥·♥·♥·

"What do you think?"

Everyone had returned to Clare's apartment after all before they'd go out together. As if reading Avery's thoughts, Clare showed the elegant gown to her when they were alone in her bedroom. Not much of a surprise that the thought of Clare in it took her breath away. Clare, on a regular basis, took her breath away.

"This is so beautiful. I don't think I have anything in my wardrobe that matches."

"Come on. You are beautiful." Clare leaned in for a quick kiss, her hand warm and tender at the back of her neck. Avery couldn't hold back the sigh.

"Thank you, but I wasn't fishing for compliments. I haven't had many occasions like this. Actually, I don't think I was ever invited to a Christmas party that fancy."

"Then it's about time." Clare's gaze was so full of affection it made her want to cry. For several reasons.

"I'll try to come up with something." No matter what Max said, she couldn't jeopardize something that was so important to Clare. Truth and ruin would have to wait.

Chapter Fourteen

CLARE

The next few days would be busy for both of them, but Clare hadn't forgotten about her determination to make time for what mattered. She wondered if she and Avery could manage a weekend out of town, rent a cottage for a couple of nights, go on a sleigh ride...

It might be tricky, but why not? Everything else was going perfectly. She and her team were making good progress, Jay and Parker were happy, her family was happy, and she was...beyond.

She and Avery had mostly spent time at her apartment. Clare didn't mind, and since she assumed that Avery appreciated the privacy, she hadn't pushed the issue. She had met one of the roommates, Max, who worked at *The Ground Floor* too, a few times.

Around Christmas would be a good time to raise the subject of moving in together. Clare already had a brilliant idea how to do it.

Avery's friends were obviously important to her, and Clare wanted to meet them, so she had suggested a dinner at her place the next time.

On her way to Avery's apartment, Clare reflected that she had expected more resistance. Or perhaps she had simply misunderstood a handful of things in the moments after that strange incident.

In any case, moving in together would be a big step, and a great way to start the new year—and take their relationship to the next level.

Tonight would be a casual dinner, everyone preparing something. Clare had brought wine and a selection of cheeses from a local deli, hoping that would make a good enough impression.

Moments after she knocked on the door, a woman about Avery's age opened.

"Hi! You must be Clare," she said with a welcoming smile. "Come on in. You brought wine, great. We have tons of food and booze, just find a seat and enjoy. Avery is almost ready."

Almost?

Clare looked down at her dark red sweater and jeans. She didn't think this occasion required dressing up? Taking a look around, she was relieved to realize that everyone wore equally casual gear. On the huge table at the end of the room, a buffet with mostly cold dishes was displayed, though the enticing smell came from the huge pot on the stove, probably soup.

"Thank you for having me."

"Of course. I'm Chantal. Let me introduce you to everyone."

"We've met. Hi, Clare."

She wondered what Max's somber expression was all about. Was there any reason why he wouldn't approve? Did he ever think he had a chance with Avery?

No. Christmas was almost here, and she'd been invited to a dinner with Avery's friends. She'd give everyone the benefit of the doubt.

"Hello, Max."

"This is Max's boyfriend Shane, Ryan and his girlfriend Haley, and my girlfriend Millie. Max, Ryan, Avery, and I are the ones who live here fulltime. The others mostly hang around and drink our booze."

The slightly indignant protest turned into joined laughter.

"Thank you. I feel like I know everything I need to know already."

"Well, not until you've tasted the soup Ryan made," Max, who seemed more relaxed by degrees, commented. "Someone check on Avery, and we can get this party started?"

"I'm right here."

Clare couldn't help the silly smile spreading over her face when her gaze fell on Avery who was only slightly overdressed for the occasion in her forest green dress and black boots.

"Hi. As you can see, I've met everyone already. You look amazing."

She lowered her voice on the last words but could tell from the indulgent gazes and mumbles around them that she hadn't been stealthy enough.

Soon they gathered around the table, and Ryan and Chantal started handing soup to everyone. Drinks had already been on the table when Clare arrived. Her wine joined the other bottles on the buffet, and after asking for her preference, Avery handed her a glass of white.

Clare noticed that a few of Avery's photographs hung on the wall. She was especially impressed with the scenes in the park that were just lovely. Avery had captured the city at night as well, her work reflecting everything Clare adored about their home.

"That was my first year," Avery said. "I didn't know anyone when I arrived, and I had only spoken to Ryan and Chantal online. But I've always loved the lights of the city, during any holiday. The next Christmas, I was no longer alone."

"You'll never be alone again," Clare promised and gently clinked her glass against Avery's. This time, she didn't care who overheard her.

·♥·♥·♥·♥·♥·

The longer the evening proceeded, the more Clare hesitated to bring up the move. She certainly wouldn't do it tonight when everyone had welcomed her so warmly. There was no doubt Avery took pride in her work, and she enjoyed the life she had built for herself, even before Clare arrived. That might be part of her hesitation.

Clare could easily afford to pay the rent for both of them, but Avery might not be happy with that arrangement. She had opted for an affordable solution and seemed to be comfortable.

Still, there was something to be said about the comfort of privacy. And Avery could always visit her friends, or they could have a dinner over at Clare's...

"You're daydreaming," Avery remarked.

"I'm sorry. Yes. But I'm pretty happy where I am right now. After the party, would you like to go on a weekend outside the city? Just the two of us?"

"Sounds like you two have had enough of an introduction to each other's circles," Chantal joked. "Do it, Avery. She's a keeper."

"Um, could we just have a moment? Thank you."

Avery's cheeks were tinged with pink, but when Chantal walked away laughing, she said, "I'd love that very much."

"Yes?"

"Yes. Everything is happening so fast...but yes. I think it would be great."

"Then let's do it," Clare decided. "Will you trust me to book something?"

"Yes, but I'll pay my share. I got my pay from the Christmas market."

So, she'd assumed right.

"Don't worry about it. I won't go overboard. I was thinking about a few days, a long weekend maybe, somewhere with a little more snow."

"That sounds perfect." The longing in Avery's voice told her that she had read her correctly. They shared a soft kiss while around them, conversations continued.

Some days, it wasn't all that hard to believe in fate.

Chapter Fifteen

AVERY

With each passing day, it was harder to imagine that a few words could destroy everything between them, the affection they felt for each other, the attraction getting more tempting by the minute, their shared love for everything Christmas.

She had to think of a gift. She had to think of many gifts.

Then, there was the weekend out of town.

Sitting at the kitchen table with a glass of wine on a night Clare had to work late, she wasn't kidding herself any longer. Clare wanted to go on a weekend getaway, Avery would go with her, and whatever was meant to happen, would happen.

It was all too easy to see how she had gotten herself in so deep. Avery might be a romantic, but she hadn't always been that cheerful. Her hope for a career breakthrough had been vanishing bit by bit. While her break-up with Chantal after a brief relationship had been amiable enough, it hadn't been easy either. Chantal had found someone new quickly.

On that cold December morning, a little over a year ago, Avery had fallen head over heels for the beautiful, elegant woman who walked into *The Ground Floor*, looking for something to warm herself up.

From that moment on, Clare Hartley had been the highlight of her days. Now, she wanted to be with Avery, and amnesia or not, a person didn't make up something like this.

Before coming up with the perfect gift ideas, she had to go shopping for a dress.

Avery hadn't lied. She didn't have that kind of wardrobe in her closet, and she didn't want to disappoint or embarrass Clare in any way.

This was an occasion to splurge, even though the extra traveling, including the weekend away, would put a strain on her finances.

It might all be over in a matter of weeks.

Just like Avery, many other residents, along with tourists, were shopping for gifts and party outfits. When she dared to step inside a boutique with higher priced offers, she found it a bit less crowded.

Immediately, a friendly employee was by her side, and to Avery's relief she didn't make any assumptions about Avery's ability to pay for one of the luxurious dresses. *Lucy*, she read the nametag.

Brenda Lee sang a sad Christmas song in the background. Avery hoped that wasn't a bad omen. But no—good things happened at Christmas, didn't they? Everything was possible. Even the idea that Clare could forgive her. She had done everything she could, and she would go out of her way to make it the perfect holiday.

"Can I help you?" Lucy asked.

It was on the tip of her tongue to say no, and flee the store, but Avery reconsidered at the last moment. "Maybe. I'm looking for a dress to wear at a Christmas party..."

There was a tiny hint of indulgence in Lucy's expression.

"An office party. My girlfriend's."

Lucy didn't bat an eye. Good. So, she likely wouldn't pay a fortune to a homophobic business. Avery flashed back to the scene on the street when Clare got angry because she couldn't join her in the ambulance. The point of no return? Maybe.

"She works at Jay & Parker," Avery added.

"Oh, really? You're lucky. The food and decorations will be spectacular."

"So I've heard."

"You're in for a treat," Lucy insisted. "Let's find you something spectacular. Would you like a glass of champagne?"

The urge to run was strong once more.

"That would be lovely," Avery said. What was one more pretense? Friends, including Max, had often told her she needed to take more chances. She was ready to lay it all on the line for the perfect Christmas memory.

·•·♥·♥·♥·•·

The cold air felt frigid on her hot cheeks when she left the store a little under an hour later. It might be the champagne—or the price she'd paid for the shiny, forest green dress without blinking. Lucy had assured her it went perfectly with the color of her hair, and when she'd seen herself in the full-length mirror, Avery couldn't help agreeing. Knee-length, with a pretty neckline. It accented her waist—and other attributes.

Avery wasn't irresponsible. She would still pay for her share of the rent, for food, the necessities of life...She'd be a lot more frugal in the coming weeks, except for when it came to the gifts for her hosts, and Clare.

But this was important, for the perfect memory she wanted to create. If there was anything she regretted, it was having missed the moment, sometime in the past year, when she could have told Clare how she felt. Some days she'd been convinced she didn't stand a chance. On others, when they had one of their short conversations that brightened her day, she'd felt like she had all the time in the world.

It turned out that neither had been true, and she had to do the best she could with that.

Chantal and Ryan weren't home that night, only Max standing by the stove stirring what appeared to be curry Ramen noodles.

"Hi. Got something fabulous?"

He was making an effort, she could tell. Avery wasn't sure if that made things better or worse.

"Usually, you're not so interested in my shopping," she remarked.

"Oh. Sorry. I thought there was a gift for me in there. Are you hungry?"

"I could eat," Avery admitted, picking up the bag again. "Thanks. I'll just put this away."

"*La Vie en Or.* You won the lottery and didn't tell us?"

"Nice try. It was on sale."

"You know I only want to make sure you don't get hurt, right?"

"I know, and I appreciate it. But I have to do this my way."

"All right then. You're the Christmas elf. Hurry up, it's almost ready."

She didn't need to be told twice.

·♥·♥·♥·♥·♥·

Avery had gone to the building most mornings in the past three years, usually to work at *The Ground Floor*. The few times she'd been on the upper floor had been in the summer, and she had appreciated the space Jay & Parker had created, modern without feeling cold. Still, slightly intimidating. When she stood in front of the mirror, taking in her tense expression, she still didn't regret her exorbitant spend for the evening.

A knock on the door startled her.

"You ready?" Chantal called. "Clare is here."

Ready? She wasn't, not for the glamorous party she was about to attend, or the weekend away, or spending Christmas with Clare's kind and generous family. But she had to be.

"May I come in?"

Clare, still in a coat and knee-high boots, stopped in the doorway as Avery turned to her.

"You think this will be okay?"

Avery wanted to stop time. She wanted to remember forever the way Clare was looking at her, her expression hiding nothing: Affection, desire...love.

"I think it's more than just okay. You are so beautiful." With a couple of steps, Clare closed the space between them, accentuating her words with a gentle kiss, her skin still cool against Avery's heated face.

"That might be an exaggeration...but thank you."

"You're welcome. Are you ready? I'm sure we will arrive in time for cocktails and canapés."

"The lady at the boutique told me this party would be a treat. I'm starting to think I had no idea."

"Well, I've been only once, but I've heard it's going to be bigger and better. I can't wait for you to see the decorations. Oh, and I totally want you to meet a few people. I'm sure they will want you to come back to work for them the moment there's an opening. Wouldn't that be fun?"

Clare's excitement was infectious. It had always been Avery's dream, long before they even met, to be with someone who found the same joy in the holidays as she did, in Christmas in the city. It was almost as if they had their own little romantic movie...Except those always had happy endings. But they had their *happy* right here and now, for as long as it would last.

"It would be, but that's not the main reason for me," she admitted. "I love everything we do together."

Clare's face lit up at the confession.

"I do too, but I think you already know that. Come on. Let's go drink my boss's expensive champagne. It's been quite the year. We've earned it."

She reached out a hand, and Avery took it.

Whatever happened from now on, they'd always have tonight.

"Always remember I love you."

She halted, startled to realize the words had actually tumbled out. Clare didn't mind.

"That's the easiest thing," she said.

· ♥ · ♥ · ♥ · ♥ · ♥ ·

On the floor of Jay & Parker, Clare unlocked her office where they left their boots and coats. "This will be quicker than the wardrobe," she reasoned.

Avery had grown quiet, taking it all in. A huge Christmas tree sparkling with an abundance of lights and ornaments stood in the lobby. She had seen another one when they walked past the party area. It was bright, and oh so merry, miraculously over the top and tasteful at the same time. A dream. That was until Clare took off her coat and changed into a pair of pumps.

Avery knew she was staring, but she couldn't help it.

Clare's dress was longer than hers, but showed lots of skin in the back, the color a dark rich burgundy, with sparkly threads woven through the fabric. In her heels, she was easily a few inches taller than Avery.

In a moment from now, she would attend an enchanting Christmas party at this woman's side. What had she done to deserve this? Okay, that was a tricky question. Luck. Christmas magic. Or a cruel twist of fate.

"Is everything all right?" Clare asked softly.

"Oh yes. It's perfect."

They left the office and walked back down the hallway to the room where the sound of chatting and laughter greeted them.

Baby Please Come Home was playing as they stepped over the threshold and into Jay & Parker's winter wonderland.

She caught Clare's gaze on her, feeling her own excitement and pride in the woman she loved, reflected. If they had made it to this moment, what could go wrong?

No, don't answer that. So, so many things.

A friendly waiter approached them with a tray, and Clare took two of the glasses, thanking him. Turning to Avery, she said, "Merry Christmas. It's going to be the best ever."

"That's what I like to hear," Jay Diaz had come to greet them. "Clare, Ms. Murphy, right? Welcome. We hope you'll have an amazing time."

"I have no doubt. Thank you for having us."

The warm relaxed atmosphere, Clare's hand on her back, and, likely, the champagne, helped with her nerves. It was going to be a beautiful night.

· ♥ · ♥ · ♥ · ♥ · ♥ ·

Avery had tried to keep her expectations in check prior to this event. As the evening unfolded, she came to realize that there was no way she could have imagined most of it. The food was excellent as everyone had told her, the decorations beautiful—Clare introduced her to a few colleagues who all seemed a bit surprised, but friendly and kind.

She was starting to think that she had overreacted labeling herself a bad person. All she wanted was to be happy, and for Clare to be happy. At the same time. That wasn't too much to ask for, was it?

When Clare asked her to dance, she didn't hesitate for a second. Being in her arms felt natural. Right. Perhaps fate had given them a little nudge, and her guilt was useless.

"I was a bit nervous about coming here at first," she admitted.

"Why? You had no reason." Clare's whisper against her cheek made her shiver. "Don't you know I'm bursting with pride introducing my beautiful talented girlfriend to my colleagues?"

"You are too kind."

"I've been better since I met you. You are the most important person in my life."

Avery wasn't the only one blurting out confessions tonight.

"I know you like your roommates, and they're nice people," Clare continued without missing a beat. "But I'd love to wake up with you every day. Move in with me?"

On the dancefloor, Avery stepped back, unable to hide her shock. A blissful one, granted, but a shock nevertheless.

"You'd want that?"

Clare smiled ruefully. "Too much?"

"No...no, that's not what I meant. This is...I wasn't sure if that's what you wanted. I've been...I swear I didn't mean to string you along."

"I know, you've had a lot on your mind. And my clumsy tumble didn't make it easier."

She reached out to brush a strand of hair behind Avery's ear.

"Just think about it, okay? It would be convenient...but also lots of fun."

"I can imagine."

"Good, that's all I needed to know. Let's go get some more champagne?"

Avery had no objections, and they made their way over to the buffet where Parker Hall was standing with a man and a woman Avery hadn't been introduced to.

"Clare. Would you mind if I steal Ms. Murphy for a few minutes?"

"No, please, go ahead. I'll go sit with Sara over there for a bit."

Before Avery had much of a chance to react, Parker Hall continued, "I was just talking to Monica and Scott about the great work you did for us. Unfortunately, we didn't have much of an opportunity to offer to you, until now."

"I know everyone loves the holidays around here," the woman said. "It can be rough for some of us who have family that don't welcome us or our partner at Thanksgiving or Christmas. We came up with the idea of something uplifting, and big for a Valentine's Day campaign. Of course, we have our own photographers here, but did I mention it's going to be big? It's going to be all about happy couples. Would you be interested?"

Once more, Avery was struggling to find her words.

Chapter Sixteen

CLARE

E verything was going according to plan, perfectly, no, better.

"You are glowing," Sara commented with an affectionate smile. "Is there something we should know?"

"What? Oh, no, not that. It's probably all the gold and silver around here—and the champagne."

She couldn't hide it though. Being with Avery, dancing with her, watching her seize an amazing opportunity...Clare loved all of it. The future was wide open, looking brighter than ever. So much had changed since her accident. The sliver of unease was gone as quickly as it had come.

No, the change had happened before, when she met Avery, and they got together. Now that her parents had seen for themselves that she was happy here, they might stop trying to convince her to move back home.

Her mind was at ease, with the job, her family, and the woman she loved. If there had been anything stressing her, holding her back before, it was all gone.

"You seem a lot more relaxed," Sara said. "A big part of it must be her doing. You were never like this when Quinn was still around."

Her comment stirred up something unwelcome, a memory Clare didn't want to deal with. An argument? Of course, she remembered Quinn, but that was a long time ago, wasn't it? Her early days in the city. It had been short, no doubt about it, because she'd had that anniversary with Avery. Why was Sara talking like it happened only weeks ago? Months?

She took another sip and watched as Avery was talking to Parker and a couple of her colleagues. Focus on what mattered. The perfect night. The days to come.

Finally, handshakes ensued, and Avery came back to the table.

"I'm sorry I left you waiting."

"That's fine. I was hoping something like this might happen, and you deserve it. I've been wishing on a star, you could say. Speaking of which, I'll come back to *The Ground Floor* tomorrow. I've been missing those lattes with the pretty art."

"I've been missing you there," Avery admitted as she sat down.

"That's my cue to give you some privacy. You two have fun," Sara advised. "Nice to meet you, Avery. Happy Holidays, you two."

There was no need to analyze what might have happened in the past, and when exactly. Happy was what mattered, and the present moment. Clare was beyond grateful to have it all.

·♥·♥·♥·♥·♥·

The evening was far from winding down. They had danced some more, tasted more of the amazing food and wine. At this point, Clare was also grateful that her dress's shape allowed a bit of space. She looked over to Avery who had a dreamy look on her face. The Magic of Christmas. Every day with her was special, but this time of the year...a bit more.

Clare's gaze wandered over to where Sara was standing with another colleague, sharing an intimate smile. Clare had to smile, too, as she remembered Sara wondering out loud if he was single.

A waiter approached the couple who looked to be in deep conversation, and for some reason, Sara turned around at that exact moment, the two of them colliding and ending up on the floor, canapés and champagne flying, the tray cluttering to the ground.

Several guests rushed to their side to help. Clare wanted to, but she felt like she couldn't move, frozen in her chair. She couldn't make sense of her reaction. It was a bit of a mess, but from the looks of it, no one had gotten hurt. They were even laughing.

Happy Anniversary!

Good luck on both fronts. Where did that come from? She saw the picture clearly though, overlaying her vision for a moment, distracting her from the commotion.

Hey, maybe we should pretend to be girlfriends. Both our parents might stop asking us to come back?

Pretend? Why would Avery suggest such a thing when they were...

The fragments were starting to come together, but the picture didn't make any sense. She started to shiver, a body memory of coming to on the cold sidewalk, in pain, even when she was warm and safe in the present.

Avery's shocked glance, her eagerness to help, her hesitation to... do what exactly? Admit they were a couple, had been in love for a year?

That anniversary. Why had she never remembered how they got together? Clare remembered the candle in the cinnamon bun. Avery wishing her well for the meeting. Other memories started flooding her mind, from last winter.

Walking by Santa's workshop, realizing that the elf was indeed the cute barista from *The Ground Floor*. A spontaneous selfie. Buying a couple of photographs for her apartment.

And then it came to her:

Until the day of her accident, there had been no kisses, no declarations of love.

Clare got to her feet so quickly her head spun, drawing Avery's attention. It was the last thing she wanted to deal with right now, more attention and concern from Avery.

"Are you okay?"

"Yes, fine." She didn't want to snap and give herself away, avoiding it barely. Clare left the room without looking back and went straight up to her office where she put on her coat and changed into her boots.

She hadn't been stealthy enough, she realized when Avery knocked on the doorframe and walked through the open door a few minutes later.

"Is everything really okay?" she asked, sounding anxious.

Now she was worried?

"You tell me." So much for not giving herself away.

"What do you mean?"

"Were you ever going to tell me?" Her voice went up a notch, beyond her control. Clare was determined not to humiliate herself to the point of crying. She was close. Memories, her real memories, came rushing in, of working long hours to secure the project that was supposed to be her pride and joy. Trying to convince her parents that her life was here in the city. Their nagging might be gentle, but persistent, and she'd been coming to the end of her rope trying to make them understand.

Jay & Parker, her bosses who were friendly but nevertheless expected results. Pressure everywhere...and then there was Avery, with the easy smile and the sweet offerings, Avery who always made time for her no matter how busy she was. Clare could always count on her for kindness, affection, and the best latte in town...

She had taken it all in until there was no way back, and she fell in love with her.

"I wanted to tell you. I tried, several times. You told me—"

"Oh, I see. It's my fault that I put myself into a situation so easy to exploit."

"Exploit?"

She didn't like putting the hurt in Avery's expression, but Clare, too, was hurt, and she couldn't find any other way to express herself.

"Clare, the doctor told me not to force your memory, that things could get worse. So, I didn't."

"And had a good laugh with your friends at my expense?"

"Of course not! Why would you even think that?" Avery didn't have the same reservations. She was crying. "Please, you have to believe me, I wanted to tell you. I didn't want to make things worse for you, and I...I'm in love with you. I have been for a long time."

"Please. Spare me."

Clare grabbed her bag and turned on her heels, leaving her standing. On second thought, she went back.

"Come on. I need to lock the office."

Avery pulled on her own boots and gathered her belongings.

"Could you please let me explain? Maybe we could grab a coffee, and talk about—"

"No. I don't see what's to talk about. I was delusional for some time, and you played into it. It doesn't make sense, but it's not something you do to a friend, let alone someone you pretend to love."

"It's our favorite season. I got so scared when you had the accident, and I wanted it to be perfect for you. I thought—"

"Don't start. Don't give me a Magic of Christmas story. The story is that you lied to me for weeks. I don't need that in my life. Bye, Avery. Don't call me."

"Clare. Please."

After locking the office, she walked away once more, not looking back until she had left the building and flagged a cab. In the backseat, she turned around to see Avery on the sidewalk, her shell-shocked expression not so different from when Clare first saw her after the accident.

How was that possible? She'd been the first there, the first thing Clare saw when she opened her eyes—convinced that Avery Murphy was her girlfriend.

If they had never been for real, why did it hurt so much?

"Where to?" the cab driver asked.

Clare gave him the address and leaned back into the seat. The urge to burst into tears was still strong, but she resisted. There was nothing to cry over—but Avery had given her a lot to think about.

·♥·♥·♥·♥·♥·

At her apartment, she went straight to bed, not even caring to take off the dress. Why, the evening had been a great success for both of them. She had received lots of praise. Avery had secured an assignment.

Clare pressed her face into the pillow and groaned. She would have to live with seeing her around, even if she never set foot in *The Ground Floor* again.

She turned around and stared into the half-dark. Snow was falling again, creating a soft romantic atmosphere she didn't care for. She could see the snow globe she had put on the dresser. One of Avery's photographs, the skyline of the city they both loved in sunset, hung on the other wall.

Avery was everywhere. Clare wiped her face. Perhaps she had to draw long overdue conclusions from that. There might be a lesson in all of this for her anyway, about whom she could trust.

Christmas never failed at giving those lessons, did it?

Chapter Seventeen

AVERY

S he'd known it would come to this. At some point in the
future. Avery hadn't expected to find herself shivering and
crying on the sidewalk in front of the building that housed both
hers and Clare's employer, at the end of what had been, up to
that moment, a glorious night.

She had barely noticed what happened with Sara and the
waiter, only that Clare got very quiet and left abruptly. She
didn't want to believe it, but when she saw her getting her coat
and boots, about to leave without telling Avery, she couldn't
deny the truth any longer.

There was no way she could have prepared herself for this
conversation. Avery knew that now. Every one of Clare's words
had cut deep through her hopes and excuses.

Avery wasn't sure how long she'd been standing on the sidewalk before another cab pulled up, and she finally got in.

"Bad night?" the driver asked sympathetically, and she nodded, not wanting to talk. Her teeth were chattering, which was,

of course, like the rest of it, her fault. She told him her address and then turned to look out of the window, but all she saw was Clare's expression, her disbelief over what she saw as a betrayal.

Was she right? Had Avery wanted this to happen so much she had abandoned all reason? Had she misunderstood the doctor on purpose?

To be fair, the woman hadn't asked her to pretend to be Clare's girlfriend. Clare hadn't exactly asked—she'd been certain, and she had refused all attempts to correct her.

At least that's how Avery remembered their interactions. Maybe she was all wrong, had been selfish beyond reason, because she'd been in love with Clare for so long.

They arrived at her building, and she paid the driver. Avery prayed that her roommates had already gone to bed or were out partying somewhere. Her wish wasn't fulfilled. She didn't see Max when she walked in, but Chantal and Ryan were watching a movie, a giant bowl of popcorn between them.

"Hey! How was it?"

Chantal turned around, her face falling when she saw Avery. That seemed to be the reaction everyone had toward her in the past hour.

"Avery! What's wrong?"

"I'm sorry. I don't want to talk about it."

Chantal and Ryan exchanged a worried glance.

"I'm fine. I'm going to take a hot bath," she announced and fled, before they could ask any more questions.

A few minutes later, the hot water finally stopped her from shivering, but by the time Avery dressed in her PJs, the warmth still hadn't made it all the way to her heart.

She didn't know what to do. Well, at least she knew what *not* to do, because Clare had told her she wished no contact. What if—Checking her phone, Avery realized Clare hadn't changed her mind and magically forgiven her.

There was no magic in the circumstances, just an unforgivable mistake. She went to her room, still reeling with disbelief. A few hours ago, she'd been truly happy. In Clare's arms. Whenever she and Clare had been in a different area of the room, their eyes would meet, Clare's smile filling her with joy. She had been so sure the feeling was mutual, that tonight might be the beginning of something...

She cried even harder when she remembered how Clare had asked her to move in. After three years in the city, her life had seemed to be on an exciting new trajectory, with the woman she was madly in love with, and new job opportunities. All of it had vanished into thin air. Even if Jay & Parker still wanted her to work on the assignment, Avery wasn't sure if she could do it.

She would have to, because a chance like this wouldn't come back, but that didn't change the facts. Wanting to create the perfect holiday, she had ruined Christmas for both of them.

Max would be too nice to go for "told you so," though under the circumstances he easily could.

·♥·♥·♥·♥·♥·

When she woke up, the sun was shining into the room. Her head hurt which was more related to her self-inflicted heartache than it was to the champagne she had consumed. Avery blinked and reached for her phone, bolting upright when she saw what time it was.

Not only had she messed up the best relationship she'd ever had, but she would also be late for work.

Avery was in her clothes and out of the house in record time. Today, her breakfast would come from *The Ground Floor* when she had a minute. Max wasn't working today which was a relief. She made it to her workplace with enough time to spare so she could grab a coffee before her shift started.

She wished Clare would come in and give her another chance.

She feared Clare would come in because Avery felt utterly unprepared for this conversation.

Was it really over? Days before Christmas?

She blinked back new tears, trying to ignore the dizziness. It might be from the strong coffee on an empty stomach and smelling all the sweet treats around her. Avery couldn't deny it. This would hurt for a long time to come, and she had no one to blame but herself.

Chapter Eighteen

CLARE

She sat at her desk, frowning at the sandwich on the paper plate she had bought on her way. It wasn't all bad—in fact, it might be a healthier breakfast than the rich cinnamon buns, muffins, and other pastries she had consumed at *The Ground Floor* in the past year.

More and more, she'd had a different reason for frequenting the coffee shop. Not anymore.

Focusing on her work hadn't been so bad. Now that she was on a break, things were indefinitely worse. She had made a fool of herself, going on dates with Avery the cute but scheming Christmas Elf, introduced her to her parents, met the room-mates...Asked her to move in. She wanted to bang her head against her desktop.

Okay, Avery hadn't asked for that, but she hadn't said no to anything, not given Clare any hint that everything between them was nothing but an illusion. Or had she, and Clare didn't want to hear it? She shook her head. No, she wasn't going to take the blame for this. She fell and hit her head. A concussion had distorted her memory, her mind struggling to work with the input she'd had at the time.

It wasn't her fault. Was it all Avery's? Clare wasn't ready to explore that question further, and she wasn't sure she ever would be.

What she needed was some distance. Relax. Reconsider what was most important in life.

Enjoy Christmas.

"You're shaking your head at a sandwich," Sara remarked. "Is it that bad?"

"No. No, not at all." She'd have to face the consequences, do the right thing. It wouldn't be easy, but it wouldn't be harder than cutting all ties with Avery either.

"I think I just need a real break."

"Well, it's coming. You and Avery will spend a few days with your folks, right? You met her parents yet?"

Clare made a non-committal sound, and to her relief, Sara accepted that she didn't want to deepen the subject.

AVERY

If she had any hope that Clare might change her mind sometime during the day, it was all gone when she checked her phone again that night. She hadn't seen her on her way in or out, and that might be coincidence, or a sign that Clare was actively evading her.

For the first time in a long time, she found it incredibly hard to stay friendly and courteous with customers who were often rushed, and not always that polite. Avery managed, just barely, exhausted by the time she left and walked to her subway station.

People carrying huge gift bags passed her by, chatting excitedly. From every side and angle, there were lights, decorations, Christmas cheers.

Bells. Another Santa.

Everything she used to love about this time of year, especially in the city she had chosen to be her home, seemed to mock her now.

Home, was it really? Jay & Parker had offered her an assignment, but Avery knew from experience that a follow-up to it wasn't that likely. She was lucky to have her friends and an affordable place to live, but that arrangement was supposed to be temporary.

Not likely.

The idea that she might fall in love again this deeply? Impossible.

Avery realized she wasn't quite past the crying stage. She didn't want to break down on a full commuter train either. She needed a plan. That had gotten her through many tough spots in her life, when she needed to find a place to live or else, when the wish for a breakthrough didn't come true.

When she got off the train, once more jostled by other passengers eager to get on and off, she couldn't help thinking a change of pace, for a few days, would have been nice.

Havenwood. She had no illusions about Clare wanting her to join her family for Christmas, but Avery knew she had to make something right. Otherwise, Christmas would be ruined for real—and for a long time to come.

·♥·♥·♥·♥·♥·

She hadn't meant to cry again while coming up with that elusive plan, but Avery couldn't help it.

"Okay, that's enough," Max who had knocked on her door a few seconds ago, decided. "There's a better way to deal with your sorrow. Let's go out for dinner? My treat."

"Oh, that sounds good." Ryan peeked inside the room. "Does that include the rest of us?"

"Yes, please," Chantal echoed. "We haven't gone back to that awesome pizza place yet, *Davina*'s? We could have dessert at the market."

Avery felt far too exhausted for all that energy coming her way.

"I don't know. I think I'd like to stay in."

"Oh, come on, You can't!" Chantal disagreed. "Honey, it's not that hard to see what happened, but if she makes you this unhappy, she never deserved you."

Max cleared his throat.

"It's complicated," Avery admitted. "It's not her fault at all."

"You're the Christmas elf. What terrible thing could you possibly have done?"

"Hey. Chantal. This is supposed to cheer her up," Max reminded them.

"I'm all for that if she gets going anytime soon. I'm hungry."

Avery managed some faint laughter at the joke. "I don't know...but...okay."

When everyone had left the room, she picked up her cell phone and stared at it for several minutes. The selfie they'd taken together. Clare's eyes were sparkling with sheer joy.

"I'm so sorry," she whispered. Her finger hovered over the call button.

"Don't do it."

She jumped when she heard Max's voice.

"Why are you sneaking up on me?"

"Give her some time," he advised. "If she was serious, she'll come around."

Avery tossed the phone on the bed. "I don't know about that. I wish she'd just hear me out. I never wanted to hurt her."

"Try to see it from her point of view. It's got to be a bit of a shock, especially since she's liked you for a long time."

He left her with what wasn't quite a big revelation, but something she had never fully acknowledged. If she had, maybe those decisions wouldn't have been so difficult—she wouldn't have tried to hold on to an illusion? Clare had liked her before the accident.

Avery picked up her phone again and called the number.

It went straight to voicemail.

"Are you getting ready?" Chantal called from the other side of the door. Avery sighed. She didn't have much of an appetite, but she had to be grateful to have people in her life who cared. She'd see her parents on the 24th as usual, and perhaps stay a couple of days longer.

Chapter Nineteen

CLARE

"You know we appreciate initiative and commitment, but frankly, you should be home by now," Jay Diaz commented, pointing to the papers on Clare's desk. "Don't tell me this can't wait until tomorrow."

"Don't let your husband hear that," she joked.

"Hear what?"

Clare almost rolled her eyes when Parker appeared.

"Ms. Hartley, don't you have a home?"

Jay snicked. "See? We're in agreement. Get out of here, get some rest, and we'll start fresh tomorrow."

That had a nice ring to it. Start fresh. Only she felt like she was stuck in her present stage of disbelief and disappointment. How could she have fallen for Avery this deeply? It had happened one smile, one kind word, and extra special latte at a time.

The end of her dream, on the other hand, had been quick and cruel.

"You're ganging up on me, I guess I have no choice."

"Say hello to Avery," Jay said. "She was gone very quickly yesterday."

"Yeah." Clare gathered her coat, purse, and keys, unwilling to deepen the subject.

"I'll wait in the car," Parker announced. "Good night, Clare."

"Good night." She turned off her computer and she and Jay walked down the hall to the elevators. A thought was forming, an idea she might have considered bizarre before, but her whole life had turned bizarre in a matter of days. They got on the elevator, and she pushed the button for the lobby, and the parking garage one for Jay. Then she blurted out:

"Jay, I think I need a favor."

"What is it?" he asked.

"I know I was supposed to work until the 24th, but I'm not sure I can make it. I need a few personal days."

"Are you all right?"

Aware of his concerned gaze, Clare hurried to explain. "Regarding my head, yes. I just need to take care of a few things."

"Is that why you stayed this late?"

That was only a part of it, though he didn't need to know that. She nodded.

"So, if it's possible..."

"Sure, whatever you need. Good night," he said as they elevator doors opened. "I'll see you tomorrow."

"Yes. Thank you so much."

"You're welcome."

Clare crossed the lobby to the front door. Once outside, she started walking into the direction of her apartment, then reconsidered and turned back. Being alone among strangers was better than being all alone.

Some stores were still open, people flocking to bars and restaurants. From everywhere, she could hear Christmas music, cherished songs. Clare remembered a time, about a year ago,

when she'd walked this same street, filled with joy and gratitude. She had made it, working for one of the most prestigious
ad agencies in the city, living in a cozy but beautiful apartment—being part of the fabric of this extraordinary place.

Back then, she didn't mind being by herself. Christmas had
been around the corner, she'd made plans to go home to Havenwood for a few days, then spend New Year's Eve with friends
and colleagues...the best of both worlds.

Clare frowned when she remembered that night, her leisurely
stroll along the decorated windows, thinking how some people had preconceived notions—that the residents of this city
weren't polite or welcoming. Her first week at work, she already
got proof that this wasn't true. She kept coming back to *The
Ground Floor*.

Even that early, Avery had been on her mind a lot.

But Avery hadn't been just a friendly face to disprove stereo-
types some of her friends from back home might have. She
had become so much more than that within a ridiculous short
amount of time, until that unbelievable betrayal. What had
she been thinking, that Clare would never find out? Even if
her memory hadn't returned, Clare had found the occasional
inconsistency. She was supposed to just live with them?

It seemed trivial to claim it was worse this close to Christmas,
but it was, because the holiday meant so much to them. Had
Avery told the truth about that, or was it all part of the ruse?

It wouldn't be the most wonderful time of the year, not this
time.

Something that held this much meaning for her, now felt
tacky and superficial.

From somewhere inside a store, she heard the lyrics of *Where
Are You Christmas*, the sentiment making her throat go tight.
Where indeed. She needed some distance, from her jumbled
feelings, from everything that had happened.

She wasn't going to find it here.

Chapter Twenty

AVERY

An evening out with her friends had been nice but didn't bring any solution. In the morning before leaving for her shift, she called Clare's number once more, expecting the call to go to voicemail again.

"Hello?"

Her heart seemed to skip a beat when she heard her voice instead. Now was the chance. Maybe the only one. Avery froze, the words she thought she had prepared, a chaotic mix in her mind.

Clare ended the call, and her chance was gone.

For the moment? Forever?

She had no idea what to do. But she had to go to work.

CLARE

S he was still in her PJs when the phone rang again. Clare was curious, but nowhere near detached when she saw the caller ID.

"Hello?"

If Avery wanted to explain things to her, she had better have a good explanation. Clare had done some research on her own—for sure it was common advice not to try and pressure amnesia patients into remembering. That went for highly traumatic experiences.

For sure, taking a header on the sidewalk hadn't been fun, but Clare wouldn't have slipped into a depression knowing they weren't together, not *yet*.

If Avery had never gone along with that illusion, if they could have started out with the truth...

Unnerved, she pressed *end call* when Avery couldn't seem to find the words. If she didn't know what to say, what did she expect?

Next, Clare brewed herself a pot of coffee and warmed the cinnamon buns she had bought, in the oven. Not as good as the ones from *The Ground Floor*, but she wouldn't set food in the coffee shop anytime soon—and not just because she wanted to avoid Avery.

When her breakfast was ready, she took a deep breath, willing herself to be grateful for the first lazy morning in months.

She called her parents' number, glad when her mother picked up after two rings.

"Hey, mom," she said, surprised at the sudden rush of emotion before she had even approached the subject.

"Clare, hi. It's good that you call. Do you know when we can expect you and Avery? You're still going to her parents' on the 24th?"

"Mom. No." *Now* it was time for that emotion. "I wanted to ask, would you mind if I came a few days early? Like, today? Just me."

Miraculously her mother could tell her state of mind from only a few vague words.

"Clare, sweetie, of course. Are you okay?"

Well, that was debatable.

"I'll be fine. I was able to get a few more days off since the project went well."

"Is Avery going to join us later?"

"No, I don't think so. We broke up."

"Oh no. I'm so sorry."

"Thank you, Mom." The floodgates were open. Clare couldn't hold back the sad truth any longer. "Avery was lying to me the entire time! We were never together. It was all pretense."

"What?" Her mother sounded genuinely shocked. "She seemed so nice. How did that happen?"

She couldn't back out now, even if that meant admitting to some omissions of her own.

"When I fell and hit my head, I lost some of my memory."

"Clare!"

"Yes, I know, I should have told you. The doctor said I'd be fine. I didn't want to worry you. But when I woke up, Avery was there, and I…I mixed something up." How to make sense of it? "She was scared. And up until that moment, she had always been so kind, and somehow, I thought that she…that we were together. I was in love with her! She cooked for me and kept me company while I was recovering. She never told me the truth, and she never intended to. I remembered."

Clare had run out of words, and there were a few seconds of stunned silence on the other end.

"Wow. That's quite the story. Why would she do something like that?"

That was the million-dollar question. Why?

"Who knows?" Because she thought she was doing the right thing—how? Because she wanted it to be true? "I have to get ready now. I'll see you and Dad later?"

"Of course. I can't wait. Christian and Shannon and the kids will be over for dinner too."

"That's great. I look forward to seeing them. Bye now."

She wiped a tear from her eye and finally focused on her mediocre cinnamon rolls and coffee. No one could have it all, not even at Christmas—but she was so much more fortunate than many others.

Spending time with her family would do her a whole lot of good and make some important decisions easier.

·♥·♥·♥·♥·♥·

Clare had never been so grateful to hear *Next stop – Havenwood* over the PA system. During the train ride, the snow had picked up, from a few flurries back in the city to something akin to a storm by the time she arrived.

125

A woman who was traveling with her teenage daughter helped her move her luggage, including multiple gifts, to the platform where her father was waiting for her.

He wrapped her in a tight hug.

"Welcome home."

"Thanks, Dad."

He took her suitcase and a couple of gift bags while she carried the rest to his car. It was snowing heavily here, fortunately only a short walk to the parking lot.

When they were in the car, he turned on the radio, only to reconsider when cheery Christmas music blasted from the speakers. Turning down the volume, he asked, "Would you prefer something else? I can also turn it off…"

"Mom told you."

"I'm sorry. We thought she was nice, but that's an awful thing to do, dumping you before Christmas."

"Yeah. Well. It wouldn't have been great after Christmas either, but in her defense, I broke up with her after…I remembered."

"It's good you did. Remember," he hastened to clarify. "It's too bad it had to come out this way. You really seemed to like her."

"I did. But I can't ignore what she did."

"I imagine it wouldn't be easy, under the circumstances. But we're glad you're staying with us a little longer. You take all the time you need. It's been a turbulent season."

"No kidding," she agreed.

· ♥ · ♥ · ♥ · ♥ · ♥ ·

Dinner in the cozy surroundings of her childhood home never failed to lift her spirits, especially around the holidays. She might not find Christmas this year, not really, but the familiarity of the place, the decorations, and her family around the table calmed her.

Clare tried to ignore the sadness mixing into that calm when she remembered the day they'd all spent together in the city, with Avery. She had fit in like she'd always been a part of the family.

She was supposed to be here.

Not anymore.

Later that night, she returned to a corner of the living room she'd always loved as a kid, partially hidden behind the Christmas tree, a cozy armchair by the bay window from which she could see the snow fall. She would read a book, snack on some candy, breathe in the scent of the fir uniquely associated with the season. Not much had changed, except now she could add a glass of wine to the mix.

Plus, adult problems and melancholy.

She almost dropped the glass when she realized she wasn't alone anymore. Clare blinked at the image of Shannon wearing an apron.

"I thought you went home."

"Have you looked outside?"

"That doesn't explain...that," Clare said pointing at her sister-in-law's outfit.

"Oh, right. I thought since I'm here, I might get a head start on the last-minute baking. Your mom graciously agreed to let me use her fabulous kitchen again. You want to join me?"

She laughed at Clare's doubtful look.

"I'm sure you have an eye for decorating, but don't worry, they just have to taste good. And there might be more wine involved."

"Now you got me."

Clare got up to follow Shannon into the kitchen where baking utensils and ingredients were already laid out.

"I missed this."

"Snowstorms? Late night baking?"

"All of the above. And hanging out with you."

She and her brother's high school sweetheart had been friends for a long time. With them starting a family and Clare working hard for her ticket out of Havenwood, and a lucrative job in the big city, they hadn't seen a lot of one another.

She should be happy. Not thinking about how much fun it would be if Avery was here...

After pouring another glass for her and Clare, Shannon started to build her dough. "I missed you too," she said. "And...I heard. I'm really sorry."

"Is there anyone who doesn't know?" Clare sighed. "It's okay. I'm trying to move on." She couldn't help thinking that Shannon's expression looked doubtful. "That's what I'm supposed to do, right? She lied to me."

"Yes, and that's no small thing. Has she told you why at least?"

"To be honest, we haven't talked much since I found out. I just...couldn't. She said something about the doctor not wanting to force memories. It's so strange. What do you get out of playing someone's fake girlfriend?"

"Maybe if you like them so much you grasp at every straw...?" Shannon mused out loud.

"Come on."

"I'm not saying she was right, just that she might have some obvious reasons."

Clare shook her head as she put all of her frustration into kneading dough. She had to admit it felt good.

"If only she had told me...We might have started dating right away."

"You fell and had a concussion," Shannon pointed out. "Maybe dating wasn't the first thing on her mind but making sure you were okay."

"That doesn't make sense. None of it makes sense."

"You still love her?"

Clare wanted to argue, but all she said was, "We'll have to get this in the oven soon. Let's cut out some cookies."

Chapter Twenty-One

AVERY

S he had a good excuse. This time anyway. She was supposed to follow up with Jay & Parker, so she could at least take care of setting up a date for the meeting. Her heart was beating in her throat when she took the elevator to the agency's floor and walked to the reception.

After she had scheduled her date, she stood for a few seconds, recalling walking the same hallway with Clare, the two of them dressed up for a magical night...

She couldn't back out now. She needed to talk to her. Even if Clare never wanted to see her again afterwards, she had to make things right. Apologize for her mistake in judgment, for her own delusions, and make her understand that she meant no harm.

And then what? Let her go? Avery wanted to flee, but she was the one who got things wrong. She couldn't afford to be a coward now.

"Avery, hi."

She turned around to see Sara smiling at her. "Nice to have you working with us soon."

"Thank you. For now, it's only a meeting, but I have some ideas." That was a lie. Valentine's Day, happy couples...Avery wasn't particularly inspired, but she couldn't share that. "I was hoping to see Clare."

Sara's face fell in a spectacular fashion, making her fear for the worst. She had heard her voice on the phone just yesterday.

"I thought you knew. She took some time off and went home early. To be honest, it was pretty abrupt. I hope her parents didn't make an offer she couldn't refuse."

"Oh...okay. Thank you. I'll see you around."

Avery didn't have time for Sara's confusion. She headed back downstairs to the lobby, where she stood, indecisive for a few seconds. Could it be true? Had Clare decided to leave early because of her? She might be overestimating herself greatly, but she couldn't take the chance either.

Speaking of chances...This might be hers to make things right, however painful it might turn out to be. If someone had to make room, it was her.

She couldn't let Clare give up on her dream when all she wanted was for her to be happy.

Avery wasn't yet sure on how to achieve her goal, but she'd never been more serious about it.

·▼·♥·♥·♥·♥·

After finishing her shift, she retreated to the pizza place she had gone to with her friends. Avery could see a few things more clearly.

Max had tried his best to keep her from experiencing the inevitable heartbreak. All of her friends had tried to be helpful, when she first arrived, recently, and at any time in between.

This was on her to solve.

While she waited for her order, Avery researched Havenwood, and how to get there. If she was lucky, she could go there and say what she needed to say and leave in time for two families to have a merry Christmas.

She frowned at the search results that spoke of a recent snowstorm, and delayed trains. She'd make it anyway. Somehow.

Her phone rang, and for a moment, she wished things weren't quite this complicated, and that Clare was ready to listen to her now.

Instead, her father was on the phone.

"Dad, hi."

"How's my favorite Christmas elf doing?" he asked, and she couldn't help laughing.

"Nobody will ever let me live that down, right?"

"Mom and I think it's awesome. You've always loved Christmas so much, isn't it the perfect job?"

"Okay, you got me there."

"You can't deny it. Avery, I hope you're not too disappointed, but your mom and I have had quite the surprise. We won a Christmas trip to Aspen."

For a moment, she was too stunned to answer.

"I thought we could come join you afterwards and stay for New Year's Eve, but we know how much Christmas means to you. We can still cancel the whole thing."

"What? No! Of course you have to go. I'll be fine. And like you said, we can spend New Year's Eve together. Not all of my roommates are going home for the holidays."

She knew that Chantal and Ryan would stay, for their respective reasons. Not everyone's family welcomed them over the holidays. She and Clare were both incredibly lucky. Why was she on the verge of...Not again.

"Are you sure?"

"Yes, absolutely! I hope you have the best time."

"Thank you so much. Mom is here. I'll hand you over?"

"Thanks. Merry Christmas, Dad."

"Merry Christmas, Avery."

She stayed a few more minutes on the phone with her mother who sounded beyond thrilled about the opportunity.

Avery pondered telling her about the assignment with Jay & Parker but decided that could wait until the next year.

"I'm so glad you understand," she said. "I feel better knowing you're not alone. And have you asked out the lady who comes to your coffee shop all the time?"

Avery sat back, stunned.

"What?"

"What's her name, Clare? You've mentioned her a lot, and she seems to like you too, so it makes sense."

If only she knew...

"It's complicated."

"Not that much," her mother disagreed. "You just have to take the risk. If they're the right person, it's worth everything."

"Thanks for the advice."

"Always."

Avery was well aware of, and embarrassed by the tears, even more so when the restaurant's owner came to her table seconds after the waitress had brought her meal.

"What's wrong? Can we help with anything?"

"No. No, I'm sorry. It's delicious. In fact, it's the best thing in my life right now."

"Please, let me know if you need anything. And dessert is on the house."

She might be embarrassed, but not enough to turn that down.

Avery ended her meal with a cappuccino while booking her train ticket online.

·❤·❤·❤·❤·❤·

During the trip, she had plenty of time to worry about the wisdom of her decision. Avery didn't think she had a choice. If she had to spend this Christmas without family, maybe it was a form of punishment, a lesson she had to learn about holding on too tightly, wanting too much.

Either way, she had to get this over with. She hadn't booked a hotel. This time, Avery wasn't going to overstay her welcome.

Why was she still afraid? Hadn't the worst already happened?

She had found the Hartleys' residence the old-fashioned way, in the online phone book, and taken a cab from the train station.

Clare's parents weren't wrong. Havenwood was a beautiful town, and its residents were going all in on Christmas. They drove past many decorated houses, one with lights in every tree on the property, another with a giant inflatable Santa. Yet another one had a more understated display of Santa with his sleigh and the reindeers.

For a few minutes, Avery could almost make herself forget why she had come here. The driver pulled into another residential neighborhood, slowing down as he drove down the street. Reality set in once more.

She was tempted to ask him to turn around but held back the impulse. She had to make something right, no matter the cost.

"Could you please wait for me?" she asked the driver who shrugged. "It won't be long."

"Sure."

"Thank you."

Then she was standing at the front door, about to ring the bell. A wreath richly decorated with lights and ornaments showed the observer that this family, too, was ready for the holidays. She swallowed hard and lifted her hand.

Before she could ring, the door opened, and she came face to face with a stunned Diane Hartley.

"Avery. I didn't expect you here." She quickly composed herself, but Avery was certain Clare had told her what happened.

"I'm so sorry to disturb you, but I need to talk to Clare. I came to apologize."

"You already did. That doesn't change the facts."

Clare had spoken those words. She stood behind her mother, her expression unreadable.

Avery couldn't help it. Her heart beat faster at the sight of her.

"I know. I was hoping you could hear me out just once. You shouldn't leave because of me, or anything that happened. I'm sorry, Mrs. Hartley, I know you'd like Clare to come home, but she's been living her dream."

Clare seemed to hesitate, giving her hope for a few seconds.

"Let her come inside?" Mrs. Hartley suggested. "It's cold out here."

Avery appreciated the support, though she barely noticed the temperature, her eyes fixed on Clare.

"That won't change anything. Avery, I'm sorry too, but I've made my decision. I'm going to stay in Havenwood."

It was Avery's turn to be speechless. Clare sounded like she had made up her mind already.

"I guess you don't know me all that well. If I learned anything from the past few weeks, it's that you don't take family for granted. I hope you'll find whatever it is you're looking for. Take care, Avery. Let's go inside, Mom."

Once more, she had greatly overestimated herself. Avery's vision blurred as she rushed back to the cab, directing the driver back to the train station.

She had been wrong—it could still get worse, and it had. Maybe Max had been right when he said to leave it alone.

Chapter Twenty-Two

CLARE

She could hear her mother talking quietly to Shannon. Clare didn't even care if they were talking about her, which was likely. She sat in the living room in her favorite spot, leaning forward as she let the tears fall.

Was this the end? Likely, because she had shut the door in Avery's face, literally and figuratively.

Was this what she wanted? As long as she had distance from the city and spent time with the people she loved, people she trusted, the decision seemed easy.

Clare almost resented Avery for coming all the way here and making her doubt herself.

She looked up to see her mother in the doorway. Her affectionate smile held no judgment, though Clare knew her well enough to know she had an opinion on the matter.

"Are you really still that angry at her?"

"I wish I knew," Clare admitted. "I am angry, because all of this could have been different, if she'd told the truth right away."

She recalled the moments when their stories didn't seem to add up. Ironic how Clare's biggest fear had been that Avery might want out of their non-existing relationship. She had cherished being close to her, sharing everything with her.

"Yes, she should have. But she also took care of you."

Yes, Avery had been by her side, cooking, cleaning, watching cute movies with her...and sleeping in her bed, in her arms. Maybe some of it had been strange for her too, and Clare had often taken liberties that seemed normal when you were with someone, touches, stealing a kiss here and there...

She went along with all of it, under the guise of what?

Because she wanted it to be true so much almost nothing else counted? Why had Clare's mind done the same—to play tricks on her?

Maybe she could find Avery after the holidays, talk to her...or she had her last chance and blew it. Avery was probably going home to spend time with her parents as planned.

The perfect Christmas she'd hoped for wasn't going to happen, or maybe Clare had fooled herself thinking that the only way it could be perfect for Avery, was with her?

She didn't know what to think or do—nothing she wanted to admit in front of her mother. Chances were she already knew.

·♥·♥·♥·♥·♥·

"Enough with the sulking," Shannon declared. "We're all leaving at four."

Clare stared at her bleakly. Time had gotten away from her as she sat and berated herself for not taking that chance. Who could guarantee that Avery would even still want to talk to her in the new year?

Where would she be?

"Where are we going?"

"Sleigh ride," Shannon reminded her, a hint of impatience to her voice. "Come on, it hasn't been that long ago."

It had been a tradition for the Hartleys and extended family for years, though the last time Clare had worked until Christmas Eve and missed it. She didn't feel much like it now. Leaving the house did not appeal to her.

"I think I'll pass this year."

"Oh no, you can't miss it twice in a row! You're here for a reason. I know you're not feeling all that great right now, but why not try to make the best of the situation? You might be in for a surprise."

"I'm not sure I appreciate any more surprises," Clare grumbled. "I just want a few days to relax and make sure I'm doing the right thing."

"You can contemplate that on a sleigh and over a hot chocolate," Shannon decided. "And if you'd like to talk, we'll all be here for you."

"We're going up to the restaurant?"

"Ah, I got you there. Yes, of course. That's part of the tradition."

The sleigh ride always led to a cozy restaurant in the hills of Havenwood where guests could sit by the fireplace and enjoy sweet and savory winter treats.

"Okay. I'll get ready."

"Great." Shannon gave her a triumphant smile. "I knew it wouldn't be that hard. You love their cheese fondue."

"You can always get me with food. Thank you," Clare said. She got up to embrace her sister-in-law. "I'm grateful you're all bearing with me."

"Heartbreak before Christmas is the worst. But you never know what can happen."

"Wait, Mom didn't invite the teacher she wanted to set me up with? She's not still coming to dinner?"

"Of course not," Shannon assured her. "How inconsiderate do you think we are?"

"Okay. Sorry."

"It's fine. Just go and change into something warmer now. We're leaving in ten minutes."

·♥·♥·♥·♥·♥·

She had to admit that when they got out of the car in the parking lot of the company organizing the sleigh rides, Clare felt a sliver of a familiar excitement. She still had a hard time forgetting how Avery's eyes had lit up when she talked about the getaway and a possible sleigh ride.

It had been a beautiful illusion. It still made her sad it was never going to come true.

They walked up to their respective sleighs. Christian, Shannon, and the kids took one of them, Clare followed her parents to another.

"Sweetie, I think yours is over there. Have fun! We'll see you at the restaurant."

Before Clare could react, they were already off. Dumbfounded, she walked over to the sleigh her father had pointed to, stopping cold when she saw who was already on it.

Her instinctive reaction was to be mad at everyone, her family, who had obviously arranged it, and the woman who had gone along with it. To Clare's surprise, resentment was quickly drowned out by relief...and something else she wasn't quite ready to admit yet. Her eyes were stinging once more.

"I'm so glad you're not the teacher," she blurted out.

"Are you going to climb in?" Avery asked anxiously. "Please. I'm probably the last person you want to see, but when Shannon came to the train station, I knew I had to give it one last try."

Clare got into the sleigh and reluctantly slipped under the warm blanket she had to share with Avery. Still keeping her distance as much as it was possible in the confined space.

"I'm trying to figure out why everyone feels like they must keep secrets around me. Am I that scary?"

"You are amazing," Avery said ruefully, then caught herself. "I'm sorry. You have every right to feel betrayed, even though it's not what I intended. But I lied to you, and I regret that."

"Apparently I didn't listen to you much." Clare sighed. As if by some magical force, or simply because of the cold, she scooted a bit closer.

"I could have tried harder."

"Yeah, you could have," Clare acknowledged. Silence settled between them as the horses pulled the sleigh through forested areas and then by snow-covered fields. In the distance there were lights everywhere. "At least you get your sleigh ride."

"I should have said something." Avery held her gaze, and Clare found herself unable to look away. "Not just after the accident. Before. You always made my day better. I wanted to get to know you so much."

"Why didn't you say anything?" Clare asked, genuinely curious.

"Things were good. I was afraid I might ruin it..." Avery's eyes were welling up. "And why would you be interested in someone like me? You're successful. You made your dream come true."

"So did you." She had to be missing a piece. "I didn't buy your photographs out of pity, and nor was it the reason Jay & Parker offered you the job. Avery, you are extremely talented." Somehow it was important to her that Avery knew that. Clare had never imagined that she might have any doubts. She had seemed so confident and happy in every aspect of her life.

"I know I'm not half bad, and I enjoy working at *The Ground Floor*. But sometimes I wondered if I had made a mistake," Avery admitted. "I thought I might never get ahead...and that a woman like you was far out of my league."

"Oh, Avery."

"The time we spent together was like the perfect fantasy, like a scene captured in a snow globe. Like one of those movies. I always knew it couldn't be real."

"Why not?"

Avery stared at her in confusion. "What are you saying?"

"Why can't it be real, when all our doubts and fears are?" All of a sudden, Clare couldn't stop, and she found the words that had eluded her earlier that day. "Don't you think I had many doubts when I first came to the city, or even after a year of working for Jay & Parker? My family is great, and still I felt like I had to prove to them I made the right decision. I had to prove to Jay & Parker that they didn't mess up by hiring me. I spent more than a few nights wondering how I'd pay for the apartment if I lost that job. Everything seemed to be easier when I could talk to you, if only for a few minutes a day."

"I felt the same."

"You always made the best of every situation, and you had a life in the city already. I admired that. Most of all, your smile always made me feel like I could really be the person I hoped to be. You looked at me like I could do anything...and I thought about asking you out more than once."

That seemed to shock Avery. "You did?"

"Of course. I wish I had...but my reasons not to do it were pretty much the same. What if it messed with the awesome thing we already had? What if you didn't want to be with me?"

"You never needed to worry about that."

"So, you're not mad at me?"

"Me? Why would I—?"

"I'm sorry," Clare whispered. "That was the last time I'll ever let you stand in the cold."

She leaned in to kiss her lips, and within seconds, neither of them was cold any longer.

Chapter Twenty-Three

AVERY

This wasn't a dream. The nightmare had been temporary, but now everything told her that they could find their path. Never again would she keep something from the people she loved because of assumptions she'd made, because of her own lack of confidence.

Chances were she could make things so much better by telling the truth. Under the warm, heavy blanket, Clare held her hand.

Avery held on tightly in return, her earlier fear replaced with hope. For the present moment. For their future.

She wasn't cold anymore. Or scared.

"I think they might have asked the guy to make a detour," Clare murmured.

"It's okay. I don't mind."

"Maybe I do a little. They might start the meal without us."

Their shared laughter made her feel happy and free. Even if she had to go back home tomorrow, she'd know Clare wasn't angry at her any longer. She would see her again, and not just to serve her something sweet at *The Ground Floor*.

Avery's cheeks heated when she imagined all the possibilities. First, they would have dinner with Clare's family though. She couldn't be more grateful for their intervention.

The ride took them through the magical snow-covered landscape, up a slight elevation, until they made it to the restaurant.

"We've come here almost every year since I was a child. Last year I couldn't make it," Clare said ruefully. "That was the day when I hung out at the coffee shop for hours after work. I really needed to be with someone kind."

"I'm so sorry I didn't tell you," Avery felt the need to repeat as long as they were still alone. "All I wanted was for you to heal and have the best Christmas ever. And for you to know you are loved."

"Well..." Clare's smile took her breath away. "It seems like all of your wishes have come true. And I love you too. I have for a long time."

Avery leaned into her embrace.

They didn't speak until they went inside the restaurant—no more words were necessary.

·♥·♥·♥·♥·♥·

Clare's family had not started without them, save for a glass of wine each of the adults had in front of them. When they came in, Clare's mother gave them a knowing smile. Shannon looked pleased with herself.

It appeared that the results of their conversation and their new-found happiness was obvious to everyone.

"You made it," Shannon said. "Did you have a nice ride?"

"Perfect," Clare confirmed. "I swear this is the last time I needed you to arrange things behind my back. I know better now, so let me do things properly. Everyone, meet my girlfriend, Avery."

She turned to Avery as if hoping for confirmation.

"I'm so happy to meet all of you," Avery chimed in. The real introduction, the one she would remember forever.

All of a sudden, everyone was talking at once, and a friendly waitress arrived. Clare and Avery squeezed into the booth next to Shannon and her daughter, and everyone finally ordered their meal.

Clare being next to her, food on the table and a good amount of the red wine gave Avery the courage to say what she needed to say.

"I wanted to thank you all so much for your help. I'm not taking it for granted. And I'm sorry for kind of messing with your plans. I swear I'll leave tomorrow, and Clare and I will sort out the rest."

"Avery, why do you think you have to leave?" Diane asked. "Of course you're welcome to spend Christmas with us as planned."

"Mom, perhaps she wants to go see her parents?" Clare gave her a questioning look. "Although, if you were able to change plans, you could stay here for a few days?"

Her hopeful tone warmed Avery's heart.

"Truth be told, at first, I thought I'd be going home tonight. Aside from that...It turns out my parents won a trip to Aspen. They are sorry, but also excited to go, and they'll come visit me for New Year's Eve."

"That's perfect, then," Clare's father declared. He raised his glass. "To things going as planned."

Not everything was, but Avery wasn't going to mention it when the most important question of all had been answered.

If Clare still wanted to work in the family business, they would make it work with the distance. Spending a few days in

Havenwood might be a bit tricky, given that she'd only brought an overnight bag and gifts she had hoped to leave with the Hartleys for Christmas. No need to mention it right now. She'd figure something out.

Clare picked up her glass and clinked it against Avery's. "And to the perfect Christmas."

Chapter Twenty-Four

CLARE

When she had rushed to leave the city and come to hide out in Havenwood, she hadn't expected that the night before Christmas Eve, she'd be sleeping next to Avery in the room she'd occupied as a teen.

Finally, the dark clouds were gone from her mind, all the uncertainties and doubts, leaving only room for the perfect bliss. By the time they had made it to the house, it had started snowing again. This time, as she lay awake, her mind was calm and clear.

She knew what she wanted, and what was most important to her.

The perfect Christmas wasn't out of her reach. It was happening.

She fell asleep sliding into precious dreams of a time when she'd been younger, certain that her wishes could come true, especially around this time of year.

She woke, still believing.

·♥·♥·♥·♥·♥·

Clare almost laughed at Avery's slightly confused expression.

"I don't blame you," she said. "This has been a lot to take in. But it's all true, and we're going to have the time we've both dreamed of."

"Thank you for summing it up for me." Avery gave her a sleepy smile. "It still feels somewhat unreal. Everything is so..."

"Magical?"

"Yes. But once again I've stayed overnight without bringing enough clothes. I didn't want to say anything yesterday, because we had so much more important issues to address, but...I might have to borrow some of your clothes again."

"That's no problem. I'm warning you that today it's jeans and ugly sweater day until dinner."

"That sounds perfect. You'll do the gift-giving tomorrow morning? Since there are still some believers?"

"You are here. *I* believe in Santa." Clare laughed. "But yes, for the kids. The adults do it in the evening after they've gone to bed, but you don't have to worry. We can do something private later."

"Will you come back to sort out things with Jay & Parker? Do they already know?"

"Not yet. I thought it might be better to soften the blow, and I needed to take that time off right away."

Avery reached out to brush her fingers over Clare's arm, the tender gesture making her shiver.

"I understand. And I didn't mean...I already got the best gift."

"Me too."

Clare pushed back the covers. "But now we need to get going before they get any ideas. I know there are some things we still have to address, but definitely not here." She winked before she headed to the bathroom, leaving Avery to blush once more.

AVERY

Sitting at the breakfast table with the Hartleys, Avery could easily see everything she had done wrong before, and how fortunate she was to still end up here.

Even at Christmas, no one's life was a scenery in a snow globe, or one of the Christmas movies she'd binge-watched with Clare after her accident.

When it happened and Clare's mind insisted that their shared dream was actually true, she had a choice and nearly ruined everything. She couldn't contain or control anyone's reaction, if people liked her photographs or not, or if Clare loved her back or not. But she did, and when Avery finally took the chance, it paid off. There was no detour, no way to know what was in the gift box before you opened it.

The fact that they'd found the courage to open their hearts and minds to each other was proof that the magic of Christmas still existed, and she found it here with a family who had welcomed her despite all.

She couldn't ask for more, could she?

In the afternoon, everyone changed from their Christmas sweaters into outfits more appropriate for the evening. Avery had been okay with borrowing jeans and a sweater from Clare, but the sleeves and hem of her dresses were too long. Shannon lent her a dress that was closer to her own size, dark blue velvet that looked like it was her own.

The family got into two cars, Clare's dad's and Shannon's, to drive to the service and Christmas concert in Havenwood's church. Surrounded by tall firs, their branches heavy with snow, it was the perfect Christmas scenery. Not long after they sat in the pew, Clare to her right, Sara to Avery's left, the church was filled to the last seat.

Avery could tell that the children were getting more and more excited, even though they would get their gifts in the morning. Rumor had it that Santa came through for children—adults gave each other gifts. Especially when they were in love.

"Are you looking forward to tomorrow?" she asked Clare's niece who had a big smile on her face.

"Oh yes. I know Santa isn't real," she lowered her voice, so her little brother couldn't overhear, "but Christmas is still awesome, right?"

"Oh yes, it is."

Quiet fell over the small church. The choir had assembled, and they took their audience through a spell-binding performance of traditional and modern Christmas songs.

Whenever Clare's eyes met hers, Avery couldn't help thinking that whatever challenges they would face, in their careers, making time to see each other despite the distance, she knew they were up to it. Together, and each of them in their respective fields.

As much as she loved interacting with customers at *The Ground Floor*, she'd try harder to find other opportunities this time. She was no longer afraid of taking chances—and she would support Clare in whatever was the right decision for her. Seeing her with her family, in the town she grew up in, Avery wistfully admitted she might know the answer already.

They still had some time together, here in Havenwood, and when Clare would come to the city to give her resignation.

They walked back to the Hartleys' house, Clare's hand in hers. Not everything might be this easy in the future, but she was beyond grateful for this moment.

As soon as everyone was out of their boots and coats, someone turned on the music, and Clare's parents went to get everyone a cocktail.

Avery and Clare went to help them, when her cell phone rang.

"It's my parents," she said, surprised. She had thought they might still be traveling.

Avery accepted the video conversation, and both her parents showed up on the screen, smiling widely.

"Hi, Avery. We couldn't let Christmas Eve go by without talking to you. Merry Christmas, sweetie."

"Merry Christmas, Mom, Dad. You're there already."

"Yes."

Behind them she could see the cozy fireplace, hear voices in the background.

"What about you? Are you having a nice dinner with Ryan and Chantal?"

"Actually, I'm here with Clare's family." She would explain everything later.

"Hi, Mr. and Mrs. Murphy! It's nice to finally meet you." Clare waved.

"Likewise. It's so lovely of you to have Avery over for the holidays."

"Oh, I'm so happy she's here. Merry Christmas!"

When Clare wasn't in the picture any longer, but still standing close by, Avery's mother commented, "Well, she's even prettier than you said."

"Mom," Avery protested as she felt her cheeks turn bright red.

"It's true! But we won't keep you any longer. You have the best time, and we'll get back to you once we know when we arrive on New Year's Eve."

"Thank you. Love you."

When she turned around, Clare asked the predictable question, "You told her I'm pretty?"

Avery saw no reason to deny the charge.

Chapter Twenty-Five

CLARE

Against all odds, she was having the holidays she'd dreamed of. Clare still had a lot on her mind as they sat in the living room after dessert, sharing a nightcap while the children were in bed, maybe not yet sleeping.

All of her wishes had come true, in no small part due to her family supporting her and understanding that she needed to be with Avery.

She couldn't turn around on her promise now, and she wouldn't.

"Hey, sis."

Christian sat on the couch next to her.

"You looked like you were far away."

"I'm sorry. I'm right here—where I want to be."

"It's a great place," he said. "I wouldn't want to be anywhere else, and I'm glad Shannon and the kids feel the same." He laughed wistfully. "As for the kids, at least now they do."

"I grew up here, remember? I like it quite a bit."

"You'd miss the city though."

"At first. Probably." Clare saw no reason to deny it. "Why, don't you want me to come work with the company?"

"You know I'd love to have you here. I had a long conversation with Mom and Dad after we met with your bosses, actually. You didn't give them your notice yet, did you?"

"Funny, you're the second person to ask me that. I'll talk to them after the holidays. You know them. They'll understand. Weren't we going to do presents?"

"Then let me go first. How would you like to work for us on a joint project with Jay & Parker? From the city?"

Clare wasn't sure she understood. "What are you talking about? No one ever mentioned to me that was even an option. How would that work?"

Her brother looked a bit guilty at that.

"The truth is, they were going to suggest it, but then you took time off sooner than planned. When you came here you were so sad, I was hesitating, in case you were serious about staying."

"I am...I was. But Mom and Dad..."

"Will make sure you'll always have a home here, in every sense of the word," her mother said. "Clare, of course we would have welcomed you back if that's what you wanted, but now that you have sorted things out with Avery, that project would be the perfect solution. We'd love to have you here, of course, but we'd still be working together on that project. We'd have to meet with your bosses every once in a while, so we could visit more often."

Avery had been following the exchange in awe, her expression hopeful.

"I mean, I'd have to look at the details...that would be amazing."

"Great!" Shannon declared. "Now's the time for champagne!"

"And adult gifts," Kevin Hartley added cheerfully. "Did I say something wrong?" he asked when he got smiles and laughter in return.

He went to open the bottle, and within minutes, everyone had their glass in hand.

"To Christmas," Diane toasted. "And love always wins."

She shared a smile with her husband, but Clare barely noticed, her eyes on Avery.

"I'm so sorry," she said to her. "I didn't even wrap anything, but I promise you, we'll still do our winter getaway. It's still in my cart, and I only have to book."

"Well, sis, you better do it now," Christian advised. "Because Avery didn't just make the trip to talk to you, she brought gifts for everyone."

Indeed, Avery had magically fit various gifts into her overnight bag, specialty coffees and chocolates from *The Ground Floor*, framed pictures of the day they'd been at the Christmas market for her parents and Shannon and Christian. One showed the kids meeting Santa, both looking equally excited.

Clare's gift was another impression of the city, showing the huge Christmas tree on the plaza in all its glory, the real-life inspiration for the snow globe.

All warm and cozy, a bit tipsy, but full of love, Clare couldn't help tearing up at what it meant.

"So, you'll come home with me?" Avery whispered.

"My home is where you are. And you'll move in with me?"

"Of course."

It was merely a coincidence that they found themselves under the mistletoe, but she would have kissed her anyway.

Maybe wishing upon that star in the latte that Avery had so lovingly prepared for her, had done the trick?

Epilogue

AVERY

When the clock struck midnight, Avery and Clare shared a tender kiss to start the new year, neither of them doubting it would be happy. After their private getaway, they were having their New Year's Eve/housewarming party at Clare's, now also Avery's home, with everyone. Avery's parents had joined them, and so had her former roommates.

"I'm glad things worked out for you," Max said after they'd hugged and wished each other a happy new year. "Even if I lose you as a co-worker and roommate, which kind of..."

Before he could finish the sentence, Clare said, "You won't lose her as a friend, and that's the most important thing, right? And she'll still be the most magical Christmas elf ever."

Avery couldn't help laughing. "That's a bit weird, but I think this was a compliment, so I'll take it."

"Please do." Clare smiled. "And expect many more."

As they watched the fireworks together, Avery knew she'd never been this excited for the future before. Not only had she found her home in the city, but she'd share it with the person she loved—and they had a lifetime of making perfect Christmas memories ahead of them.

About the Author

Barbara Winkes writes sapphic crime drama and Christmas romance. She loves writing characters who get the job done, whether it's stopping a predator or saving cherished traditions—while still making time for love. She lives with her wife in Quebec City.

barbarawinkes.com

Also by Barbara Winkes

Bells Will Be Ringing
A Girlfriend for Christmas
Christmas Cupid
Destination Christmas, Next Stop Love

www.ingramcontent.com/pod-product-compliance
Lightning Source LLC
Chambersburg PA
CBHW022126170626
46808CB00002B/854